Secret Covenants

Secret Covenants

Faye Thompson

www.urbanbooks.net

Urban Books, LLC
300 Farmingdale Road, N.Y.-Route 109
Farmingdale, NY 11735

ISBN 13: 978-1-64556-746-2
EBOOK ISBN: 978-1-64556-747-9

First Trade Paperback Printing February 2026
Printed in the United States of America

10 9 8 7 6 5 4 3 2 1

Distributed by Kensington Publishing Corp.
Submit Orders to:
Customer Service
400 Hahn Road
Westminster, MD 21157-4627
Phone: 1-800-733-3000
Fax: 1-800-659-2436

The authorized representative in the EU for product safety and compliance
Is eucomply OU, Parnu mnt 139b-14, Apt 123
Tallinn, Berlin 11317, hello@eucompliancepartner.com

Secret Covenants

by

Faye Thompson

"A good marriage is the union of two good forgivers."

—Ruth Bell Graham

Chapter 1

"You know what? This is crazy." David Dante jumped out of bed and fumbled for his pajama bottom in the dark.

"David, I'm sorry." Chantel tied her robe and smoothed her hair into place.

"Sorry?" As he shot her a look, the diamond-encrusted wedding band that he had placed on her ring finger two weeks earlier caught his eye.

"When we were dating, you couldn't keep your hands off me. Now you wanna go all Sweet Polly Purebred. I don't know how long you expect a man to wait to make love to his own wife." He pulled a T-shirt over his head before leaving the bedroom.

Chantel sat up. "Where do you think you're going?"

"To sleep on the couch." He slammed the door behind him.

Chantel threw a pillow in his direction. "David, wait. Come back."

The next morning, David and Chantel pulled into his reserved spot in the church's parking lot. He turned off the engine and stepped out, stopping to have a brief conversation with one of his members. Chantel took a quick rearview glance. She released the glove compartment and quickly unscrewed a flask. After another quick glance, she filled her empty coffee mug and snapped the compartment shut, bathing her throat in vodka. Her lips curled into a smile as David wrapped up the conversation and walked around the back of the truck to open her door. Chantel adjusted the signature single strand of black pearls that she always wore around her neck and took one last look at herself in the mirror. She then placed her hand in his as she exited the vehicle.

"You really need to lay off the booze," he whispered in her ear, his hand on the small of her back. "It's barely ten o'clock and you're already wasted. I don't care how many mints you suck on."

"Don't start. I am not in the mood," she warned through clenched teeth.

"Listen, I don't need my first lady smelling like a brewery. End of discussion."

They walked a few steps in silence before climbing the stairs into the sanctuary's vestibule. The deacons whisked the pastor away to his office, and an usher escorted the first lady to her second pew seat as the praise team rendered another selection for the Lord.

Bubbles Legree woke up early Sunday morning to give her husband's suit a good pressing. She idled on the edge of the bed, too tired to move. She wanted to leave him, but reality always brought her back with a bang. Everything was in Hayden's name, from the house that never felt quite like home to the savings account he called a nest egg. So publicly, she smiled at the appropriate times and praised the Creator for blessing her with this devout, God-fearing husband who knew scripture but not kindness. On the surface, she loved marriage and its sanctity, but after ten years of getting her behind kicked, she was ready for life, liberty, and the pursuit of her own damn happiness. The problem was that she was in no position to declare her independence. Not yet. So, she padded her kiss-my-ass account with unemployment checks. Something or someone better was bound to come along.

Bubbles' marriage was sealed by the spirit of fear—fear of being an old maid, fear that she was running out of time, fear that nobody else wanted her. Bubbles had done what any desperate woman would do in a leap year: she chased Hayden until he caught her. After tying the knot, she soon learned that the only thing worse than being married to the wrong man was wishing that you weren't, and Bubbles had the undercover bruises and overly made-up black eyes to prove it. Had she known all that beforehand, she would have remained single.

She glanced back at her husband and rolled her eyes. Running a hand through her short, ginger hair, Bubbles sighed. She slowly opened up the ironing board in her cramped bedroom, praying that the creaking didn't disturb his sleep. Next, she plugged in the steam iron, allowing it to heat up before she reached for his dark suit and began ironing on the reverse side. Hayden hated shiny spots, yet he was too cheap to send his suits to the dry cleaners.

A quick check of his pants pockets revealed a neatly folded twenty-dollar bill. Another set-up. *Fool me once.* Rolling her eyes, she squeezed the nape of her neck and winced in pain, her dislocated shoulder a souvenir of the first and last time she took his money. Bubbles obediently slid the bill back into his pocket. As if on cue, his snoring grew louder. Even asleep, he was as sleazy as slime. Her eyes plunged daggers into his back, silencing him.

"Ouch." Bubbles burned her finger and slid her thumb into her mouth to avoid blistering. She checked the watch on the nightstand as she finished up. Four more minutes of sweet peace. She savored each minute, squeezing out every last bit of tranquility before insanity awakened.

The alarm intruded her thoughts, and Hayden jumped up.

"Turn that damn thing off." He rolled over and faced her, picking the matter out of his eyes. Hayden reached up and grabbed the belt of her robe, pulling her toward him.

Bubbles frowned, hating the sight, taste, and scent of her husband. She disrobed and prepared herself for another episode of pavement-pounding sex. She eased back on the comforter, willing her mind to take her elsewhere as her husband had his way. Afterward, she made a mad dash for the shower, allowing the water and steam to wash away her husband's touch and residue.

Hayden abruptly cut short her cleansing ritual, pounding on the bathroom door. Bubbles turned off the water, wrapped a towel around her body, and walked out, avoiding eye contact. He followed and twisted her arm.

"Selfish bitch. You know how I hate losing my religion on Sundays."

"And the other six?" she mumbled.

He tightened his grip until she cried out in pain.

"You're two seconds away from another beatdown. What did you just say?"

"Nothing."

"If you had half as much money as you do mouth—"

"I wouldn't be here with you." She broke free.

Bubbles and Hayden finished breakfast. With his elbow on the table and his chin in hand, Hayden was suddenly in awe of his wife. Her freshly done eyelashes set off a flash of rhinestones each time she blinked. Bubbles softened under his gaze, flattered by his admiration.

"I'm just sitting here trying to figure out why your makeup always looks like a do-it-yourself at-home project. I married the damn before picture. Show me the after. Now, that Sable can light up the room without hitting the switch. Why can't you be more like her?"

"'Cause you ain't no Price."

His lips turned up in disgust as he took a step back. "Hold up. I know you ain't going out in public with me looking like that." He shook his head. "Must be out your damn mind. Go fix your face."

An hour later, the Legrees occupied Church of the One Way's third row pew. Hayen draped his arms lovingly around his wife's shoulders, giving her an affectionate squeeze from time to time. In return, Bubbles gave her husband a smile reserved solely for him.

Sable Galore appeared, swinging Bubbles' mood. If there was anyone Bubbles hated more than her husband, it was Sable Galore, and on any given Sunday, she could add a galore of reasons to the list. From the top of her pixie-cut 'do to the soles of her bunioned feet, Bubbles despised everything about Sable—from her effortless beauty and salon-quality hair to her perfectly pedicured toes. Sable, not Bubbles, had been Hayden's first choice for a wife. Bubbles had been number two. So, Bubbles got him the old-fashioned way. She got pregnant. After she miscarried, she was stuck with no way out.

Her eyes swept in envy over Sable's turquoise suit, but it was her matching pumps that nearly took her breath away. Those shoes, those shoes. Bubbles' lips parted ever so slightly. Damn that Sable, always dipped in diamonds and runway ready. Why was Sable always on the up elevator while Bubbles was heading down?

Bubbles dropped a tissue, giving her a reason to lean forward and get a better view as she scooped it up. Bubbles glanced down at her own pumps, badly in need of new lifts. She rolled her eyes and grabbed a fan from the back of the pew in front of her, opening it up with one quick whip of her wrist. Her eyes betrayed her, landing once again at Sable's feet. Fanning with a vengeance, she guided her attention back to where it belonged—on the Word. Again, her traitorous eyes returned to Sable's outfit, and the gnawing sensation in her gut worsened. *Focus, Bubbles, focus.*

For a few fleeting moments, she did, but like a serpent, the crystal on Sable's nearest shoe winked at Bubbles, tempting her down a wicked path. The sister sitting next to Sable leaned over and whispered something in her ear. Bubbles' chest tightened as Sable crossed her legs, looked down at her pumps, and smiled, flirting with her feet. As usual, Sable sucked up all the energy in the room, as though she hadn't a care in the world. If she only knew that Bubbles had placed a tracking device on her husband's car and had hacked into his phone . . .

Bubbles slid a stick of gum into her mouth, its minty sweetness calming as her breathing became one with the gum. Bubbles stole another look. Those pumps were dope. She tried looking away, but Sable's shoes sucked her in. Bubbles memorized those shoes, etching every detail in her mind. Were they turquoise or teal? Praying to the shoe gods, she hoped to track them down. No doubt they were out of her budget, but she had to have them. Why should Sable get all the shine? Time for Bubbles to start walking on water, too. Just as Bubbles had found a way to cheat with Sable's husband, Bubbles decided that somehow, some way, she would find a way to get those turquoise-teal crystal stiletto peep-toe pumps.

***

After service, Chantel got out of the car first and escaped to the bedroom. David retreated to the family room and turned on the TV. He grabbed a bottle of beer from the minibar and unscrewed the top, guzzling his way to the recliner. David loosened his tie and unbuttoned his shirt. He was about to stand and check the air conditioning, but Chantel's entrance forced him back into his seat. Her body blocked the TV just long enough to be annoying. Chantel's short silk robe caressed her nakedness. She gave him plenty of time to survey her generous curves and fresh Brazilian before closing up shop.

Annoyed, David looked right through her, but his photographic memory captured every inch of her bangin' body. Slowly, Chantel strutted over to the fireplace and reached for something high on the mantel. Standing on her tiptoes only further defined the beautifully sculpted calves, thighs, and bottom that topped his wish list.

Nothing but a damn tease. Disgusted, he rose to his feet, drained the bottle, and left the room.

"So, what the heck is going on between you and my twin?" Megan asked David, raiding the fridge when she stopped by one day after work.

"What chu mean?"

She turned to face him. "It's colder than a mug up in here. Honeymoon over so soon?"

"We're just going through a dry spell. That's all."

"Dry spell my behind. Y'all still newlyweds. Y'all should be banging like a screen door on a hot summer day."

"Yeah, well, tell that to her."

"Look, I don't care what nobody says. Life is all about that one person who sets your soul on fire, that one person your eyes seek out when you enter the room. That's it.

So, if it ain't your wife, you both better be some doggone good forgivers, 'cause I know you both 'bout to break all kinds of commandments up in here. But you ain't heard that from me."

Later that night, David reached for their wedding photo and flashed back to the day he and Chantel met. He was lunching alone at a table for two. As he bit into his fish sandwich, he looked up, and their eyes met. She, too, was alone. She was the first to look away while he continued to admire God's gifts from across the room.

Her skin was the color of banana ice cream, her hair a waterfall of wavy caramel locks that dangled well below her shoulders. She sipped from her water glass, then set the glass on the table, and their eyes met once again. She reached into her purse for lipstick and blindly applied it to her bottom lip like a seasoned pro. As she stood to leave, she answered her phone, laughing softly. With her left hand, she fluffed up her luscious mane, giving him the perfect shot of her bare ring finger. She took one last look in his direction before exiting.

David was about to stand to follow her out but then sat back down. For the next few days, he spent his lunch hour across from the restaurant, sequestered in his car, anticipating her arrival. Not until the following week did the butterscotch beauty strut across the parking lot while he bit into a wrap.

He wiped his mouth with a napkin and hurried inside.

She sat at the same table as before. This time, when their eyes met, he manned up and walked over to her table.

"Excuse me, miss. You got me in a trance. I can't stop staring—"

"I see you droolin'." She laughed, and he did too. "Why don't you join me?"

"Oh, you got jokes." David sat, feeling her candor.

"Nah, just good eyesight," she admitted.

David reflected on their wedding day. He had stood at the altar as the doors to the church opened. Chantel appeared on her father's arm. The sight of his rib walking toward him was an out-of-body experience and nearly took his breath away. As a newly installed bishop, David's father had officiated over the nuptials, making the ceremony that much more special.

The day's excitement had evaporated into a shockingly icy night as David lay in bed, waiting to make love for the first time and consummate their marriage.

Chantel slipped out of her negligee and slid her ripe body between the sheets. "I can't." She reached for her robe. "I'm not even the first lady type. So, let's make a deal for appearances' sake. I'll portray the perfect first lady in public and play your game, but in return, behind closed doors, you'll play mine."

David fast-forwarded to the present. What had changed? What turned a sexy, passionate woman into an ice princess? David prayed for wisdom. Something had to give.

Across town, Sable Galore was spending yet another night alone in her California king. She removed her eye mask and stretched. She turned on the lamp and reached for the iPad on her nightstand to scratch her midnight itch with shopping. She was instantly drawn back to the pair of strappy sandals that had been parked in her cart all day. She drummed her fingers on the screen, debating whether she really needed another pair of shoes or if she just needed some good loving from her husband. Something had to give. She clicked pay.

Later, Sable sat in her large open kitchen in the dark and drained her second glass of red wine before pouring a third. The sound of Price's Jag rolling into the garage instantly had her looking at her stainless-steel appliances and clocking him in at 1:37. Sable walked over to the sink and washed the wine glass by hand before placing it in the rack to dry.

Price entered the kitchen and wrapped his arms around her waist. "Oooh, it's good to be home." He kissed Sable from behind before slipping a mink collar around her neck. "It's from our new collection. Sorry I'm late."

She turned and plunged her tongue into his mouth as he tightened her collar and promised to do better. After a quick shower, Price joined her in bed. They made love, and Sable fell asleep in his arms.

Chapter 2

Sable Galore had a million and one reasons why she had refused Deacon Hayden Legree's marriage proposal. Her plunging necklines and love of salsa and merengue were not only the Pentecostal church's worst nightmare, but his as well. The deacon might have looked innocent on his way up the ministerial ladder, but she saw straight through to his Machiavellian core. She knew there was a lid for every pot. She just didn't want his covering hers. Besides, her grandmother had taught her to start out the way she wanted to finish, so she crossed Hayden off her list and married Price Galore, affluent businessman and the self-proclaimed next Long Island multimillionaire instead.

She and Price vibed right away, and why not? They wanted the same things in life—mainly a posh lifestyle in Baldwin Hills with no crumb snatchers. So, they made a pact on their wedding night. He'd focus on the former, and her newly fitted diaphragm would handle the latter. That was nine years ago, and she still didn't breathe the same when they were apart.

Sable had squealed with delight when she glanced out her kitchen window on her last birthday and saw the fully loaded E350 convertible neatly wrapped with a big white bow parked in their patterned concrete driveway. She had affectionately nicknamed her Midnight and warned other drivers about getting too close as she took her first joyride with Price by her side.

Working part-time as a restaurant greeter at Caliente gave Sable a reason to dress up and pop the top of her favorite lipstick three seasons out of the year. Since Price and the owner, PJ, were best friends, her schedule was fluid. Nights, weekends, and summers were a breeze.

Sable's morning started like most others. He wanted to know her plans for the day. She had a list of things on her to-do list, mostly for taking care of his needs and maintaining their household.

"Oh, and babe, don't forget the charity auction's tonight."

"Sable, you know I'm swamped at work. Can't we just skip it?"

"Uh-uh." She frowned. "The foundation's raising funds for childhood diseases. Let's do it for the kids."

"Okay." He exhaled. "What time does it start?"

"Eight."

"All right," he told her halfway out the door. "I'll be home by six thirty."

True to his word, Price was home just as Sable stepped out of the tub. Smiling, she wrapped her body in the thirsty towel, which he promptly removed.

"The kids can wait." He grabbed her from behind and began to unzip. "Bend over."

She wiggled free, grinning. "I owe you one. There's some jewelry I want to bid on tonight, so we can't be late."

"God forbid." He shook his head and zipped up.

"Our next item is a pair of diamond and pearl cluster earrings from the House of Marchella De Amor. Bidding begins at five hundred dollars. Do I hear five hundred? Five hundred?"

A man in front raised his paddle.

"Five hundred from the gentleman in the white shirt. Do I hear five fifty?"

A woman in the rear bid.

"Five fifty. Do I hear six? Six hundred from the lady in black pearls."

Sable looked around. It was the first lady.

"Six fifty? Six fifty? Going once?"

Sable raised her paddle.

"Six fifty from the lady in tan. Seven hundred? Do I hear seven? Seven hundred from the lady in black pearls. Do I hear seven fifty?"

Sable raised her paddle.

"Seven fifty from the lady in tan."

By now, the other bidders had dropped off, and only Sable and Chantel remained. As if watching a tennis match, Price and David had their necks on swivel.

"Eight hundred? Do I hear eight hundred?"

Chantel perked up.

"Eight fifty? Do I hear eight fifty?"

Sable's paddle flew up.

"Nine hundred? Do I hear nine hundred?"

Not to be outdone by Sable, the first lady bid.

"Going once? Going twice?" The auctioneer hit the gavel. "Sold to the lady in the black pearls for nine hundred dollars."

During intermission, the two couples met up and shared a laugh.

"Babe, you remember Pastor Dante and Lady Chantel?" Sable said.

The two men shook hands. "Please, it's David and Chantel."

"Now, Chantel, you got the earrings without a sweat, but I don't know if you would've stood a chance with my wife had it been shoes," Price joked.

"Price, I can see them now. Going at it like two chihuahuas fighting over the last pair of pumps in the shoe department," David joked.

"And guess who'd foot the bill?" Price joked.

"No doubt," David agreed.

"Listen, I am not leaving here empty-handed. So, if you're up for another challenge . . ." She looked at Chantel.

"I'll pass." She laughed.

During the second half of the auction, Sable bid on an all-inclusive trip for two to Jamaica—and won.

"We've circulated enough money for the night," Price said, taking Sable by the hand.

"Let's get outta here before we have to take out a second mortgage on our homes," David agreed.

They ended up at an all-night diner, recapping the evening's events. The husbands sat next to their wives in the booth and waited for the server to return with their orders.

"First Lady, if you had seen your face when I overbid you. Girrrl . . ." Sable teased.

"Honey, I looked across the aisle and thought, wait a minute. I know my church member ain't outbidding me on my earrings. Not on my watch."

She laughed, and the others joined in just as the server returned with their drinks. "I have a beer for you," he told Price. "And a ginger ale for your lovely wife." He placed the glass in front of Chantel. "And for—"

"No, no," Chantel corrected him. "That's his wife," she said, referring to Sable.

He moved the glass to Sable. "My apologies. Here's your iced tea, and, sir, here's your Coke," he added, referring to David.

"No problem," David said.

"We might have to wash dishes in here the way you two cleaned us out." Price felt for his wallet.

"Lord, have mercy. You two are something else." David looked across the table at Sable a second longer than appropriate.

"Women always get what we want. Right, First Lady?"

"Amen," she agreed. "But you need to start calling me Chantel, 'cause something tells me the four of us will be hanging out a lot more often."

Price and Sable were the first to arrive at Romans Ate. They were escorted to a table, and the server filled their glasses with water. He left two menus, both covered in verses from the eighth chapter of the Book of Romans. Price looked up as David and Chantel walked through the door.

In no time, Price and David were shoulder to shoulder, eye to eye. "Good seeing you again, man," Price said.

"Been a minute," David agreed, the ice broken.

"Chantel, you are wearing those earrings," Sable exclaimed before they all sat.

"Girl, I can't get over that watch. Somebody must really love you," she insisted.

"That he does," Sable agreed.

"Price, you have excellent taste," Chantel told him.

"Thank you." Price smiled as the women engaged in small talk.

The waiter returned with two more menus. David looked around at the incoming crowd. "This is some grand opening. I think this place is going to be a hit."

"You're right." Price nodded.

"And you can order takeout," David added.

Sable's ears immediately perked up. "Did someone say takeout?"

Price leaned into David. "My wife is the takeout queen."

"Oh, babe. I'm not that bad. I cook."

"Of course you do, just not in the kitchen," Price joked.

"Stop it." She laughed, feigning embarrassment.

"Girl, it's all good," Chantel told her.

"Better than good." Price reached for Sable's hand and brought it to his lips as he studied the menu. "I'm starving."

"What looks good, babe?" Sable leaned into him, sharing the menu.

"You do." He kissed the tip of her nose.

Two hours later, they capped the night with wine and dessert. By evening's end, the Galores and the Dantes were eager to get together again.

The next morning, a last-minute rescheduled GYN appointment had Sable scrambling to put on her Fitbit as she headed to the garage. Sable gazed down lovingly at her fresh pedicure and stilettos before sliding behind the wheel and driving off. Shoes were like boyfriends. They were all her favorite at one time or another. It came with estrogen.

With one eye on the road, she fumbled in the glove compartment, past the umbrella and other essentials, for her spare bottle of perfume. If there was one thing she hated, it was being without her favorite fragrance. Without it, she was only partially dressed, which was completely unacceptable.

Sable snapped shut the glove compartment and concentrated on the road. On a summer morning that rivaled any postcard, Sable's blackberry locks rippled in the warm, seductive breeze.

She checked the gas. She had less than half a tank. Sable pulled into the gas station's full-service island and waited, no attendants in sight. She got out of the car and headed toward the pump. Looking around, she spotted Pastor Dante and walked toward him as he began pumping gas. She caught his eye. He instantly smiled, and the two met halfway.

"God bless you, Sister Sable. How are you?" He wiped his hands on his dark sports jacket before giving her a church hug.

Sable returned the hug, wishing she hadn't worn such a sheer top. A whiff of his aftershave went straight to her head, and she wiggled free. Her heart pounded as heat danced across her flushed cheeks. She thanked God for the black saucer-sized shades that shielded the windows to her soul, as well as for the fact that he was riding solo.

"Is your wife still enjoying my earrings?"

"Oh, you got jokes."

"Audacity too. Pastor, would you do me a big favor and pump my gas?"

"Of course, Sister Sable. Let me wrap this up, and I'm all yours."

Though traffic was heavy, she arrived home that evening in time to start Price's dinner. Luckily, he wasn't a picky eater. Her mother had taught her as best she could. Takeout did the rest. Price knew her talents didn't lie in the kitchen, and he never complained.

Materially, Sable wanted for nothing, even though she longed for the days when she had more of Price's attention and less of the nights when her calls went to voicemail. But she'd learned a long time ago about asking questions when she wasn't ready for the answer.

Sable heard Price's Jaguar XJ as the tires rolled up to their two-car garage. The car door opened, then shut.

"Hey, babe, I'm home." Price wrapped his arms around Sable from behind and gave her a quick peck on the cheek. "Something smells good."

"Hungry?"

"Starving," he told his wife as he headed upstairs to shower. Then, he turned mid-flight. "You'll never guess what happened today."

"What, babe?" she asked, reaching for a bowl by the dish rack.

"I stopped at a light, and a car pulls up next to mine. I glance over, and it's Chantel."

"Okay . . ."

"But the funny thing is, I swear she was flirting with me."

"You sure? Maybe she was just being friendly. You know how some first ladies are."

"Sable, I'm a grown man, and I know when I'm being hit on."

"Okay, so what happened next?"

"The light turned green, and she sped away."

"And did you give chase?" Sable joked.

"Know what? This is the last time I warn you about another woman having the hots for your man."

"Oh, you mean like Bubbles?" She instantly regretted her words.

"Look, for the thousandth time, I'm sorry for sleeping with Bubbles. That ended a long time ago. She was just a release. That's it. Now, Sable, you said you forgave me. But if you're going to throw it in my face whenever the mood hits you . . ."

"You're right," she admitted, shaking her head. "I was wrong to bring her up, and I apologize. Besides, I can't fault her for having good taste. Look, if we weren't already married, I'd want you, too."

Sable couldn't blame women for wanting her man as she recalled the day that Price walked into her life. She was working at Brooks Brothers in Manhasset, and he was shopping for new suits. She took care of his every need that day, and the following week, he asked her out to lunch. She politely declined, but Price was persistent. Unaccustomed to rejection, he would not take no for an answer.

After three rejections, he changed his strategy, choosing instead to completely ignore her each time he entered the store. Not only did Sable miss the attention, but she missed the commission as well. Soon, she changed her game plan, willing him to ask her out one more time.

For their first date, Price took Sable to an upscale steakhouse in Manhattan, famous for its surf and turf. When the check arrived, Price's wallet was nowhere to be found. Sable whipped out hers. The meal had put her within four dollars of her card's limit. Sable shook his hand good night at the door and ignored his calls for a week. She never came out of pocket again.

That Thursday, she invited Price to the trendiest Latin club in Midtown. For hours, she scoured her closet for the look that would cause Price to lose his mind. Sable rocked the lowest-cut vegan leather halter dress and the highest stilettos she owned, confining her feet to ice buckets for days later. But that night, nothing else mattered except the way the drape of the dress glossed over her hips and thighs as they danced the salsa and merengue till dawn.

She could never have worn that outfit with the deacon. She'd had countless heated exchanges with Hayden about how man judges the outward appearance, but God judges the heart. The more they dated, the harder it had become to hold on to her peace. Price was another animal altogether. She could be herself with him, and she always felt at ease in his presence. No matter how bright the lipstick or how short the hem, he appreciated her. His one request was that she tone it down around his parents.

Every Achilles has a heel. Sable soon learned that Price's was alcohol. He had balls of steel and, according to his physician, a liver to match. Sable wasn't looking for perfection. In Price, she saw endless possibilities, and she wasn't about to let another woman try on his last name. She'd help get him to his next level.

After three months, she decided to step it up. On a Monday morning, she ignored her growling stomach and made a special trip to the bank, barely making it back to work on time. That night, she invited Price over for the first time.

The mischief in his eyes matched her own as she beckoned him inside. She wore a short red silk robe and the afterglow of a hot bubble bath.

"Ooh, you smell good," Price whispered in her ear as he hugged her close and untied her red silk robe.

She grabbed him by the tie, which she had helped him select, and led him into her bedroom. Disrobing by candlelight, she glimpsed herself in the mirror wearing a black satin bra and thong. Zumba classes were paying off. She helped Price strip before they both made their way over to the white down comforter, which adorned her queen-sized bed.

He covered her body with kisses before sliding a finger inside her panties. Removing her lingerie, he gasped. Sable had strategically pinned freshly minted hundred-dollar bills to the inside of her bikini and bra. The combination of Sable's scent mixed with the aroma of new bills went straight to his businessman's head. Price nearly lost his mind, bringing them both to a crazy climax.

Once Price left that night, Sable stopped taking his calls, cutting him off cold. Price blew up her phone twice a night for a week, only to get her voicemail. Finally, she took one call, explaining to him that her schedule was tight and she couldn't fit him in. He insisted that he needed to see her that evening.

"I'll see what I can do, but I can't make any promises," she recalled telling him. "Maybe we can see each other once a week."

"Once a week?" he repeated. "Hell, did you say once a week?"

"I'm really busy, Price. I have a lot on my plate right now."

"Then we have a serious problem, Miss Richards," he said straight up. "I need you in my bed every night."

Price proposed the following week. Six weeks later, they eloped. Her parents weren't pleased, but they got over it. Price and Sable honeymooned for two weeks in Rio before she settled into his home on Long Island. Price's world revolved around Sable's, and all she wanted to do was please him. But after their first lover's quarrel, Price arrived home that night with a little turquoise gift box from that iconic New York landmark store.

After that, whenever she felt sad, angry, depressed, neglected, or whatever, she'd reach for his plastic and go shopping. If she gained five pounds, she'd shop. If he was working late and she was home alone, bored to the gills, shopping became her something-on-the-side. She spent many a night putting it on his Black card when she would rather have been putting it on him. Online shopping, mall shopping, or boutique shopping—retail therapy was the answer to whatever ailed her. The power of a purchase calmed her nerves like nobody's business. It became her vice of choice.

Every month, she held her breath for the day when Price's American Express bill hit. She made sure that Li'l Miss Fix-It rocked a fresh Brazilian before she put it on him good that night and then prepared breakfast the following morning. What more could she ask for? She was the luckiest woman in the world—for another month.

Chapter 3

Price Galore had learned a long time ago that men live by status and women by beauty. That's why he worked so hard to maintain an opulent lifestyle. Sable mixed the high with the low and knew how to look like a million without breaking the bank. She worked it just as effortlessly in The Limited as in Dior, but as her husband, his job was to keep the consistent stunner in the latter.

Sable was his crown jewel. From the moment they met, he recognized Sable for the priceless instrument she was, patiently waiting to pluck her heartstrings and her body just so until she quivered. She had once confessed that he was the only man who had ever made her cum, and he had no reason to doubt her. Price would do anything to please Sable. With two successful fur salons and a new Go with the Faux discount fur line in the works, he lived by two mantras: A satisfied wife never cheats, a pampered puss never strays. He made love to her when she needed it and screwed her when she demanded it. Sometimes, he was her Raheem DeVaughn. Other times, he was her Musiq Soulchild. In return, Sable made her husband's Mondays feel like Fridays.

Except for one point of disagreement. Price had no use for Christian cliques the instant he turned legal. He steered clear of any function with a whiff of church, save for weddings and funerals. Watching some manic sister's music-induced temper tantrums after she bolted from the altar was the clincher.

As far as he was concerned, Sable was his missing rib. All the other women were just spares. And though a skeptic when it came to God, he did worship the almighty dollar. Price's self-worth was directly proportional to his net worth. God had nothing to do with his existence or his success. Price was the center of Price's universe.

He didn't mind Sable going to church. Hell, he found it comforting to know that she was trying to live right. Maybe her banked prayers and blessings would benefit him someday. Building up a line of credit with God never hurt—just in case.

He would never forget his first date with Sable. Her long, sleek, jet-black hair and her dewy, Nutella-brown skin put him in a trance. At five feet ten inches, she was a fine glass of wine he was thirsting to taste. Her body had to look like two scoops of chocolate ice cream underneath that dress, but it was her mind that had him sprung.

As they dined at the restaurant, he appeared genuinely shocked over his misplaced wallet. What she didn't know was that their dinner was already paid for, and that even the waiter was in on Price's "test." Sable paid the bill without batting an eye. But when he refunded the tab and she maintained her peace and decorum, he knew that she was rare.

He had no choice but to wife her up. He proposed two weeks later, saying farewell to bachelorhood and random lady licks. Price hadn't regretted his decision for one minute. Sable was the boss everywhere but the bedroom—or at least he let her think she was.

Price worked well into the evening before racking up another sixteen-hour day. He checked the time on his iPhone as he placed a call to his wife. Sable picked up right away, just as he knew she would.

"Hey, baby," he began.

"Don't say it. I can hear it in your voice."

"I'm sorry. I am up to my earlobes in work."

"You said that last night," she reminded him.

"I know. I'll be home as soon as I can. Trying to wrap things up for our vacation."

"Shall I wait up?"

"No, baby," he told her. "Get some rest. I'll wear you out later."

Sable laughed softly before hanging up. He locked up the office and headed for the garage. If he hurried, he could still hook happy hour. Juice's Jiggle Joint boasted the best happy hour in Westbury, and women came in droves. If a man couldn't find a woman there on any given night, he had left his balls home.

Price was a platinum card–carrying member of the private gentleman's club and had no intention of changing his status. Besides, a little dash of jealousy spiced up the sex and kept her on her toes. Sable was no fool. She knew he had a weakness for alcohol, porn, and boobs, and Juice's boasted all three. But as long as he took care of her needs and maintained their lifestyle, Sable looked the other way. Price couldn't help it if women came up to him. He had it going on. As a six-footer rocking a six-pack and making six figures, of course he was in demand.

Less than half an hour in, a young hottie joined Price at the bar. Hanging on his every syllable, she barely covered her "pow" in a dress two sizes too small. Price wasn't impressed, though. She might have been sitting on a gold mine, but with her month-old, down-to-the-ground weave, short, upturned nose, and over-plucked eyebrows, she was just another tarnished shawty searching for a sugar daddy.

"I've been watching you since you walked through the door." She tossed her hooker hair.

Little girl, not even with hot sauce. She was too damn thirsty and too young to know that modest is hottest. He preferred to chase it.

"Oh, really." He took a sip of his blackberry martini, his eyes riveted to the stripper lying on stage, pleasuring herself with a mammoth sex toy, her boobs boasting their own zip code.

"Yes, really," she continued.

"And what is your name?" he asked her.

"Chardonnay." She sat just a little straighter.

"Chardonnay," he repeated. If he had a dollar for every girl named Chardonnay, he could play golf all day. "And where are you from?"

"Texas."

"Texas," he repeated, not missing the Southern twang but nearly missing her boobs. Apparently, everything wasn't bigger in Texas. His eyes shot to the twins working the pole.

She tossed her hair as his attention wandered back to the stage. "And if you buy me a drink, I'll tell you how I got my name."

Squinting, Price looked past her to the beauty who was entering Juice's. Exquisite. He stood and buttoned his jacket as Chardonnay sucked her teeth.

Don't hate the testosterone. Hate the game. Price needed a closer look. He gulped down the last of his martini, but the beauty turned as he gave chase.

From behind, she resembled a café au lait version of Sable. He imagined two scoops of banana ice cream under those flowing tan slacks and the cream-colored halter top that maxed her S curve. He was feeling the whole monochromatic look. Not missing an inch, he glimpsed her profile as she quickly hopped into the back seat of a waiting Uber. Matte gold sandals, a freshly done creamy white pedicure, and a matching pearl ankle bracelet set it off. Dewy, sun-kissed makeup gave her skin a natural glow. Her hair, neatly coiffed in a long, sleek ponytail, lent an air of relaxed sophistication as she returned his wicked grin before the Uber drove off.

"Damn," Price said under his breath. A real baddie, First Lady was polished like a dime. Though he was more than ready to dip his stick in her banana puddin', he loved a good cat-and-mouse and could be patient when life demanded it.

He slid into his Jag and started the ignition, feeling like he was being watched. He peered through the darkness, and there she was. Bubbles Legree was clocking him through a pair of binoculars. Crazy bitch. He had cut her off years ago. Yet, she hung on. At this pace, it wouldn't end well for her.

When Price got home, Sable was in the en suite, enjoying a candlelit bubble bath. He didn't know if it was the sight of her soaking or a flashback of the first lady at Juice's that was causing his hard on, but he put it to good use.

"So, you're home." Sable smiled, extending her leg as she lathered up with a puff.

He removed his jacket, undid the top button of his shirt, and loosened his tie. She rose up to greet him, dripping wet and not caring how her body soaked his brand-new dress shirt. She kissed the tip of his nose and wrapped her arms around his neck as he eased her back onto the giant soaking tub's edge. Price feasted on the fruit between her thighs. His tongue toured her body until he had her panting like an animal.

Sable yielded to the warmth and extended one arm to steady herself. Finally, she pushed him away and stepped out of the tub. Her body took his breath away each time he caught a glimpse of it. She knew how to keep him hard. After eight years of marriage, she still checked all his boxes.

Except one.

He kissed her hard before releasing her to unzip his pants. "Come on, baby girl. You know what I want."

Sable's mouth slid from his to his chest and below. He stroked her head and whispered gently, "You got this."

She looked up and apologized with her eyes first. "I'm sorry, honey. I can't." Sable stood.

"Dammit, Sable, I should not have to wait eight years for my wife to go down on me." He grabbed himself. "Hell, this ain't no random dick off the street. I'm your husband." His voice cracked. "All of my needs should be handled in-house, and what about marriage is honorable in all and the bed undefiled?"

"Don't you dare quote scripture to me," she said, the vein in her neck popping.

"You know something? I could eat you six nights out of the week, and you'd beg for seven. It's all Sable, all the time. Right?"

"Price?" She turned the one syllable into two. "I'll do anything else," she promised, returning to his side.

"Fuck it." Patience was a virtue, but his was out the door.

"Honey, wait," she pleaded, but Price was done.

Sable cried her eyes raw before collapsing onto the cold bathroom tile.

Price had spent the past five nights in the den, while their marital bed grew colder with the dawning of each new day. She couldn't handle six. She had to settle. Runway fierce and blinging like his queen, Sable shot one final glance in the mirror before heading out the door. She'd surprise her husband and take him out to lunch like she used to when they first started dating.

Seconds from Midnight, she stopped. Her outfit screamed spoiled diva boss bitch, not the image she wanted to present to her husband while asking for his understanding and forgiveness. She turned around and returned to her closet in search of something more humble. *Tone it down, Mrs. Galore.*

Replacing the bling with creamy white pearls helped to center her, along with the lilac-colored classic sheath dress and sling pumps. With her humility leading the way, Sable greeted Price's secretary before walking into her husband's office and closing the door behind her.

Price looked up from his desk. "Sable, this isn't a good time." He stood, his jaw tight. "I'm up to my neck in work right now."

"We need to talk, Price. It can't wait," she began.

"About what, Sable?"

"You know what."

"And you think this is the place for that?"

"You haven't spoken to me in a week."

"Unbelievable." He returned to his chair, shaking his head. "You can't handle a week, but you expect me to be patient with you for nearly a decade. What's wrong with that equation?"

"Honey," she said, tilting her head to the side as she sat across from him. "You're right. I adore you. I'm so sorry. I never want to see that look in your eyes and know that I put it there." After eight years of checking all his boxes except one, she allowed those tears to drop.

"Sable? It's okay," he said, handing her a box of tissues.

She cried even harder. "No, it's not. My husband's not happy with me."

"Not the tears, Sable. Shit." He never could handle her crying. He stood and walked to her side. "Come here," he said, taking her into his arms and gently kissing away her pain. "Don't you know I adore you? Look at me."

She couldn't meet his gaze. He held her face in the palms of his hands until she did.

"I worship the ground you walk on. Sable, the day you became my wife, you made my life. No matter what we do or don't do in the bedroom, I'm hooked. You may drive me to the den occasionally, but that's as far away as I'm going. Okay? And because I have the patience of . . . what's his name, Job?"

"What you know about Job?" She brightened, her hand on her hip.

"I know a little sumthin'. I had a couple of Bible classes under my belt before I started playing hooky," he admitted.

"Not you?" She suddenly laughed.

He kissed the tip of her nose. "As I was saying, I have just enough patience to believe that one day you'll make him the happiest li'l man alive too."

Smiling, she went over and locked the door before meticulously clearing his desk. Price stood behind Sable and unzipped her sleeveless lilac sheath. Lingerie was the next to go. She undressed her husband first with her eyes, then with her hands until he, too, was naked.

Easing her back onto the desk, Price smiled.

"What are you thinking?" she whispered in his ear.

"About the night I wrapped these creamy white pearls around your neck and slipped these studs in your ears."

"Our first wedding anniversary. I remember that night well. Very well."

"I never tire of seeing my wife in pearls. And I never tire of making love to you, of sliding my tongue inside you."

An hour later, they got dressed. Price buttoned his French-cuffed shirt and hopped into his trousers before knotting his tie and sliding it up to his throat. "That's all I need to make it through my day."

"That and a new desk blotter." The wet spot they'd just made hadn't escaped her. She tossed her hair to the side as he rear-ended her and zipped up her dress. She zipped up his fly and grabbed her purse.

"I'll be home early for round two, baby." He blew her a kiss.

She gave him a wicked grin and something to admire as she walked out, though his last box remained unchecked.

As good as the loving was with the missus, Price still couldn't get the first lady out of his mind. She had taken up residence and was living rent-free in his mind. Women had too much damn power, and most didn't even know it.

He woke up the next morning, relieved that it was Saturday. He brushed his teeth and washed his face before heading downstairs in his pajamas. He planned on working from home until noon, and then, running his usual errands—to the car wash, the gas station, and to his favorite barber. He knew Sable would take care of the dry cleaners and the liquor store.

Price popped a K-cup in the Keurig before poring over the morning paper. He called out to his wife but didn't hear any reply. To make sure, he got up from the kitchen table and checked a few rooms. As much as he loved his wife, it was nice having the house to himself for a change. Savoring the silence, he grabbed his coffee mug and headed to his office.

Price breezed through his to-do list in half the time and then debated calling his partner, PJ Diggs. He and PJ had been like brothers since childhood, and they'd been best men at each other's weddings.

During his junior year in high school, when a chubby-since-birth Price met his chemistry tutor, a hot senior whose reputation beat her to the boys' locker room, he began working out at the gym to better his chances with her. Batting her bodacious Latina eyes, she had jokingly told him one night after an intense study session that she liked her men tight, and that if the day ever came when she could squeeze less than an inch on his body, she'd grant him total access to hers.

Price wasn't sure if she was serious or high, but he wasn't about to take any chances. Hitting the gym and seeing no results, he called PJ. PJ introduced him to an off-the-books personal trainer whose jailhouse-style workouts were legendary. With the Latina as his muse, gym rat Price chiseled his physique in record time. Sporting a six-pack two months later, Price passed the chemistry Regents. That night, a buffed Price banged the Latina and kissed his virginity goodbye.

Secrets came with a price. He and PJ shared too many graveyard confessions to count. If he scored with Chantel, they'd have one more to add to the vault. Yet, Price had kept one incident from his college football days, even from PJ. Not a day went by that he didn't relive the pain of that moment. Sometimes Price drank to remember, other times to forget the fateful night he learned how life changes on a dime.

Chapter 4

Maybe it was because he only had one testicle, but Adonis Watson could not smash enough cookies. Grinning, he took one last puff of his cigarette before shooting it curbside. On second thought, he picked up the smoldering butt, ground it out with his slightly run-down shoe, and placed it in his pocket. Adonis had spent too much time in the slammer to allow even a whiff of his DNA to land him back in the Tombs. The only thing Bare Hill Correctional did for him was transform his malnourished mug into a buffed, body-building thug. Three hots and a cot or not, he had no desire to return. The former pill-poppin' party boy laced his GED with a master's degree in street psychology that hadn't failed him yet.

He watched as his next mark dodged across the busy New York street, definitely a native. No doubt she could flip a car with one hand, and that was cool. He liked a dash of vinegar in his greens. She was a giant, no-neck Milk Dud, but she strutted like a queen, even on that scorching June morning. He sized her up. She was five foot four and no more. From the width of her behind, she'd been sitting on it way too long, and she had to be craving a breeze under the long red sundress that housed the rain forest between her thighs.

Adonis waited until their paths crossed before uttering his trademark pickup line. "Excuse me, young lady. Do you mind if I beg, borrow, or steal a little bit of your time?"

He put his legendary dimples to good use. And though he was badly in need of a shave, he hoped that the gleam in his sleep-deprived eyes sparked a flame in hers. What he lacked in looks, he made up for with his gift of gab.

Tootsie White blushed, displaying her pearly whites. Apparently, she wasn't used to male attention, but all women craved a little shine.

"Free country," she told him, shrugging as he fell into step by her side. They walked a few moments in silence before he introduced himself.

"I'm Adonis. Adonis Watson. And you are?" He extended a hand she didn't accept.

"I didn't say," she said, looking straight ahead.

"Well, nice to meet you."

"Whatever."

"I think I saw you a couple of Sundays ago in church," he said, reckless with the truth.

"Wait a minute." She stopped and turned to face him. "You go to One Way?"

"Sure do." He met her gaze and made a mental note to lock in the location in time for Sunday's service.

"I knew you looked familiar." She fell back into step beside him.

"Are you a regular?"

"Hmmph, I'm there every Sunday and twice during the week."

"Oh, so you're one of those sisters who don't miss a beat. Or a meal either," he added under his breath.

"What's that?" She gave him a suspicious side eye as beads of sweat formed on her short, upturned nose.

"I said I could use a meal."

"Oh, okay." She laughed. Now they were back on sunny ground. "So, what made you choose One Way?"

"The music ministry," he admitted, "but I love the way the pastor breaks down The Word."

"Yeah, he's pretty good, but I still miss Pastor Stevens."

"Me too," he agreed. "One Sunday, he was there, and the next he was gone. So, what happened to him?"

"Early retirement," she said simply. "Bad back."

"Oh, that's too bad."

"Yeah, a pastor's gotta have a strong back to baptize my crew."

"I feel ya." He licked his lips ever so slightly, displaying a chipped front tooth and botched dental work, then he bit his bottom lip. "But I like 'em thick. Real thick."

Her expression said it all. He'd already scored, nothing but net. Hell, if she'd been thin, he'd tell her he liked 'em light and tight. Hell, he made it up as he went along. Whatever a woman needed to hear, he delivered. Made no difference to him. Women loved BS wrapped in a pretty bow. Presentation was everything. Present it right, they're yours all night.

"Well, Tootsie, I will definitely see you Sunday." Adonis signaled for an approaching dollar van. He was feeling her grateful smile. No need to look back as he hopped in and found a seat.

As a veteran, Adonis had to make up for lost time. Injuries he had sustained from a landmine had put Mr. Happy out for seven years. It also cost him one of his testicles. His biggest fear in life was being sterile—though doctors insisted his fear was unfounded. His compensation claim was denied more times than the law should allow, but he was relentless.

Instinctively, he grabbed his manhood, which he affectionately nicknamed Mr. Happy, to make sure he was still intact as the driver turned a corner. After all Adonis had been through, Mr. Happy was just tickled to be alive. Mr. Happy needed lots of attention from the ladies, and Adonis was determined to deliver.

Adonis liked anything with a pair of breasts and a behind. A pretty face was just a bonus because the only thing that really mattered was the garden between their thighs. Ninety percent of men were biding time until they could tend that garden. The rest who said that wasn't the truth were lying.

Adonis readjusted his singular sensation. He specialized in the "M& Ms"—the married and miserables. He considered it his duty to service the needs of the world's M&Ms, but the church's M&Ms kept him so busy, he rarely had time to tip elsewhere.

Adonis had joined some of the most popular churches in New York, most for a hot minute or two. He had to keep moving. He could usually tell by just one visit if the women were Mr. Happy–worthy.

The dollar van dropped him off right in front of his building, and Adonis climbed the stairs two at a time to his third-floor walk-up overlooking Hillside Avenue. The first thing he did was remove the tight, phony wedding band that graced his finger. He was as single as a dollar bill but always got more action when he sported a wedding ring. Women were such suckers. He played separated, but he even kept an engagement ring stashed away for emergency purposes.

Adonis checked his messages. His editor had left two. Her getting antsy waiting for his manuscript was getting on his damn nerves. Adonis was writing a juicy tell-all about church women called *Cheat Like a Lady, Snatch Like a Man*. Females were a shady crew, every last one of them. Church women liked it nasty—the nastier the better. Their sanctified shouts and hallelujah hats didn't fool him. Catholic school taught him that even nuns had dirty habits. One first lady liked fellowshipping with Mr. Happy in the back pew while her husband taught Tuesday night Bible study in the basement. A soloist barely out of her teens always wanted it on top of the piano because when their bodies hit the right notes, the chords made her cum faster.

Between the two of them, Adonis and Mr. Happy had done it all. Almost. Adonis refused to do it on the altar. Once, an evangelist begged him to do it to her on the altar by candlelight, even threatened to have him arrested for impersonating her husband in the dark, but he refused. The altar and the pulpit were holy ground. Just because he was a sinner didn't mean he was ready for Hell.

Adonis grabbed a beer from the fridge and plopped down on the couch. He already knew there was nothing on TV, no need to pick up the remote. He flipped open his laptop, ready to write, but the words just would not come. He had been battling writer's block for too long. Adonis had assumed that with all his adventures and sexcapades, writing a book would be a piece of cake.

Maybe the problem was that he was between women and needed some new M&M juice for inspiration. He contemplated calling someone from his earlier chapters, but he couldn't afford the drama—and there was always drama at the end. Adonis made sure he put it on his conquests so good that they were hooked at first hump. He wasn't conceited. He was just keeping it real. But when he gathered enough material on his subjects, he cut them off cold turkey, severing all ties clean and quick. Sure, they'd blow up his phone during the withdrawal period, but eventually that passed, leaving them with just one more reason to cross their legs and fan themselves in church as they recalled getting Mr. Happy.

Adonis got up and headed for the kitchen. He always wrote better on a full stomach. Ramen noodles and leftover chicken would have to do. He added a can of green beans to the mix, and that was dinner.

An hour later, with his belly full, Adonis was raring to go. He wrapped up the chapter on Sister Wellington from Greater Mount Friendship Hope Tabernacle, smiling to himself at the recollection of her friskiness. Sweet piece. Just as Adonis reached for a cigarette, his landline rang. He checked the caller ID: Giselle Wolfson, his editor. He wasn't feeling her, so he allowed voicemail to pick up instead. What editor called after business hours anyway? Maybe she wanted a piece of Mr. Happy, too. Screwing himself into her wallet sounded tempting, but she was so not his type. Then again, her bird's nest could be a real sleeper. Adonis had inked a two-book deal with his publisher a year ago because of Giselle. A little flirting goes a long way, but he had yet to produce his first draft. Now, she was short on patience and thin on time. Adonis stripped and took a long shower, hoping that the pulsing of the water against his skin would pound out Giselle's tone. No such luck. She was like a nagging wife without the benefits.

On Sunday morning, Adonis shaved, showered, and suited up for church. He needed a few more chapters to round out *Cheat Like a Lady, Snatch Like a Man*. Smiling at his reflection in the mirror, Adonis stroked his goatee. He could smell a virgin a mile away, and Tootsie's cherry was his at hello.

Chapter 5

Missionary Lilly White wasn't always right, but she was never wrong. She could have written the Bible all by herself, if God had only asked.

She spread coconut oil all over her face and was good to go. That was the extent of her daily beauty routine. Special occasions warranted a pinch of sanctified brown foundation, but those days were rare. She didn't believe in makeup, but no one knew that her left pinky toe was painted as scarlet as O'Hara. Hmmph, nobody's business but hers and Jesus'. Makeup was the devil's war paint. It had sent many a woman straight to Hell, and she wasn't about to be caught dead there. Having come from a hometown with more churches than streetlights, she kept her hemline long and her patience for nonsense short.

Lilly headed for the kitchen. After all, breakfast was the most important meal of the day. Then again, so were lunch and dinner. Her mind was always at least one meal ahead. She reached for the cast iron skillet to fry bacon, hoping the aroma would wake up her daughter, Tootsie. Nope. That child would sleep her life away. Just because Lilly sat on her behind all day didn't mean she wanted her daughter to do the same. Besides, Lilly was allergic to work. She had toiled enough for four lifetimes—time to sit back and collect a check. Nothing was wrong with her that an aspirin couldn't cure, but the city didn't need to know that. Nobody's business but hers and Jesus'.

Lilly had barely passed her GED exam and preferred to keep life simple. Her diet and vocabulary remained in the same category—limited. She rarely ate anything she couldn't pronounce and nothing more exotic than French fries or Italian sausage passed her lips. A trifecta of sugar, fat, and salt—aka yummy, yummier, and yummiest—ruled her hypertensive lifestyle.

She scrambled four eggs, adding a pinch of grated cheese to "health it up." No calcium deficiency here. Finally, she popped two slices of bread into the toaster to go with the bacon and eggs, whipped up some coffee, and scarfed down her breakfast. She was itching for a nap, but Jesus was waiting.

Lilly hurried back up to her bedroom, her feet barely leaving the ground. It was time to get dressed. Her G cups had seen better days. She strapped on her white cotton brassiere, juggling her breasts for perfect nipple placement. Then she stepped into her underwear and slid into white stockings before holding her breath to squeeze into her girdle. She purposely bought girdles one size too small for maximum results, but Lord help her when she had to take it off. She reached for the powder puff and applied one more dusting of baby powder to her chest. Lilly grabbed some bobby pins off the dresser and pinned the salt-and-pepper bun that she was rarely without to the back of her head and smoothed back her widow's peak. Then she slipped into the ankle-length skirt and matching jacket. Thank goodness for its opaque lining—no need for a slip on such a muggy early June day.

Returning to the living room, she gazed lovingly at the framed marriage certificate that hung on the wall.

She checked her watch, the watch her late husband had given her on their last anniversary. That was thirty years ago. It nearly squeezed the life out of her ever-expanding meaty wrist, but the gift had come from the heart. That reminded her that time was a-wasting. She could have polished off two breakfasts. She just couldn't depend on Tootsie for a ride. Where the heck was that church van? It was after nine thirty. Didn't they know Jesus was waiting?

Lilly arrived in church just after the responsive reading. Luckily, she wasn't ushering that morning, so she could afford to be fashionably late. She adjusted her hallelujah hat as she waddled down the church catwalk, following the usher's lead. Lilly sat in her usual fourth pew aisle seat. If all eyes hadn't been glued to that silk-suited heifer, Sable, as she strutted in, they would have noticed her nearly-new gold shoes.

Lilly fanned herself to the rhythm of "Blessed Assurance." Heaven help her if she had another hot flash. Her jacket was already clinging to the nape of her neck. Apparently, the church had financial problems, but did they have to simulate Hell to prove it? As much as she tithed, she'd have to take up the issue with the pastor—again. This didn't make no kinda sense.

She looked around for her daughter, Tootsie. Where in the world was that child? Always late. The van had made three other pickups before arriving at church, and she still beat her daughter there. Tootsie raised Lilly's blood pressure faster than a plate of macaroni and cheese. Why, she once slapped Tootsie so hard that to this day, she only had partial hearing in her right ear. Tootsie's brother had escaped Lilly's clutches years ago, and they hadn't heard from him since. She loved both her kids equally, but life forced her to keep a tighter rein on her daughter. That was the price one paid for having a girl child in such a wicked, wicked world.

Humming, Lilly glanced to her right. Sable thought she was all that, but her husband barely knew what the inside of a church looked like.

Lilly side-eyed Sable's rock. Carats didn't count—kids did. That barren hussy wasn't fooling nobody.

Lilly turned her attention back to the service as the praise team sang another selection. Lilly joined in. She was no American Idol, but apparently, neither was the praise team leader.

By sacrificial offering time, Tootsie had yet to arrive. Lilly reached inside her purse, found a ping pong-sized ball of money, slowly extracted a ten-dollar bill from the bunch, and then put it back. Five dollars would do just fine because she was saving for a tummy tuck. The other day she caught a glimpse of herself without a girdle in the mirror. Lord, have mercy. Her gut-to-butt ratio boggled even her mind. She shuddered at the recollection. She needed that surgery real bad. She could barely bend and stretch to clip her toenails, let alone polish her prized pinky toe.

Gambling wasn't saintly, but it padded her stash. That's why she never played the numbers in her own neighborhood. Ever. Hmmph, nobody's business but hers and Jesus'.

Tootsie walked in right before Pastor Dante's teaching, squeezing in between two deaconesses. Lilly gave her daughter "the look," which she had first used on a five-year-old Tootsie when she fibbed about eating the last bit of banana pudding. Tootsie refused to meet her gaze, lowering her lids instead. Some things never changed.

Lilly frowned as Pastor Dante stepped up to the pulpit, looking like the Caped Crusader in his black-and-red robe. She could not get used to this new pastor, and she saw no reason to try. He was no closer to getting her stamp of approval now than he had been six months ago. He hadn't done anything wrong, but what had he done right?

She so missed Pastor Stevens. People were still blowing up their *hellephones*—gossiping about how she and Tootsie had broken Pastor Stevens' back during double baptismal dunkings one Sunday. That didn't make no kinda sense.

Lilly turned her attention to the First Lady Chantel. She and the pastor were polar opposites. Next to her late husband, Pastor Dante was probably the luckiest man on the planet. Lilly hoped that he appreciated his Eve. That woman didn't have an arrogant bone in her body. From her latte satin skin and thick, long lashes that framed her gentle browns, she made others feel like each of them was the most important person in the world. She wore a red portrait–collared suit with matte gold buttons. Her long, layered medium brown hair was swept in a neat updo, and of course, she wore those signature black pearls. Even in eighty-degree heat, the first lady was cool and poised.

Lilly was not really listening to the teaching. Her eyes roved around until they settled on Tootsie. Born Lillian Marie White, Tootsie was just as big-boned as her mother—but with twice the mouth. When Tootsie was happy, life was beautiful, but heaven help everyone and everything within a two-mile radius if so much as her eyelash was distressed. She had nearly split her mother wide open during delivery and was just green enough to keep Lilly on her knees. What she lacked in street smarts, she made up for in attitude.

By the time she was seven, her daughter had developed an obsession for that famous chocolate candy with the brown-and-white wrapper. The name stuck, and Lillian became known as Tootsie from that point on. Tootsie was almost as wide as she was tall, giving the appearance of a virtual square. Lilly reminded herself not to worry. Some men liked 'em thick.

Lilly checked her watch. How long would Pastor Dante's sermon last? This didn't make no kinda sense. She closed her eyes and began counting—slowly. God answered her prayer at one eighty-four. Maybe she'd play that number too.

After service, Lilly caught up with Tootsie. "Daughter, you're in a awful big hurry for someone who got to church late."

"Meeting some friends for brunch, Mama."

Lilly grabbed her wrist. "Well, I'll need you home in time for dinner. Understand?"

"Yes, ma'am." She wiggled free.

Lilly watched her child flee, then quickly slipped toward the rear of the church to steer clear of Deacon Greer. He was a nice man, but booze and pews never mixed. Every Sunday, he went out of his way to track her down and make a connection. When she spotted him ahead of her, she edged to the other side of a pillar, hoping to block herself from his view.

Too late. Deacon Greer's knowing smile assured her that he had spotted her too. With his eager, long strides, the distance between them was cut in half. She gave him a two-finger handshake, which he turned into a hug. Before she could stop him, he had planted a kiss on her cheek.

"Missionary White, you smell good. What you wearing?" he asked her.

"Saturday night bath," she told him.

They both laughed.

"That was some sermon the Pastor preached," he said.

"That it was," she agreed briskly. "Good seeing you, Deacon."

"Same here." He smiled as she walked away.

No need to catch the church van home. Lilly was intent on getting to the bus stop and catching the first bus going down Springfield Boulevard. She could stop in plenty of bodegas along the way to play her numbers and cash in her winning ticket from the other day. Unfortunately, just as she stepped outside the church, she was interrupted again. This time, Missionary Collins wanted to have a word.

"Lilly, I'm glad I caught you. Have you scheduled next month's meeting?" Maureen asked.

"Not yet," Lilly told her.

"Oh good, 'cause I'll be away on vacation the first two weeks in July. So, if you can schedule it some time after that . . ." Her voice trailed off.

"I can't promise you anything," Lilly said stiffly, feeling her nose begin to sweat. Time was a-wasting.

"Oh, Lilly, be a dear and see what you can do. You know how the board welcomes my input."

Lilly reached inside her purse for a tissue to dab at her nose. "Not now, Maureen. I'm in a hurry."

"Can I drop you off anywhere?" the missionary asked.

"No, no. I'm good."

Okay, but remember I'll be on vacation—"

"Got it." Lilly stole another glance at her watch. Could she make it?

Lilly hurried to Springfield Boulevard, eager to put distance between her and One Way. Just as she looked back, a bus zoomed by. The next one wasn't scheduled for another twenty minutes, so Lilly took off running. Her bus-chasing days were never really behind her. Huffing and puffing, she boarded the crowded bus, plopping down in the first available seat.

Lilly waited until she was a decent distance from the church before signaling a stop. She knew the area well. The bodega was just up the block, but in the hot sun, it might as well have been three blocks away. Trickles of sweat slid down her face. Wheezing, she pushed open the door of the bodega and walked in.

The scent of fried eggs and cheese churned her nostrils, but a working lottery machine was all that mattered. She said a quick prayer, then gave the owner her holy-oil anointed list of twelve numbers—one for each of Jesus' disciples. Only after she double-checked them did she pay him.

She had been holding back her wonderful surprise. She slid her three-day-old winning ticket over the counter for redemption. She hid the gleam in her eyes well as the owner gingerly counted over five hundred dollars, placing them in the palm of her hand. Lilly was relieved that the store was empty of customers. She divvied up the money into two halves and slid them inside her bra cups.

Just as she left the bodega, she nearly tripped over a homeless-looking man sitting a few feet away. She had a good mind to write to the mayor and the city council with some suggestions. Something needed to be done. She paid her taxes. That had to count for something.

"Watch it." She readjusted her winnings with both hands as she scurried away. His forehead housed a hideous scar that Lilly would not soon forget.

Lilly couldn't wait to get home and remove her already compromised bra. Sooner or later, a hefty jackpot was in her future. She sniffed her winnings one last time before returning the wad to its final resting place—an already stuffed shoebox underneath her bed. At this rate she'd have enough money for a tummy tuck and a bonus cut, too.

Come on, Mega Millions, Mama needs a new pair of boobs.

Chapter 6

Tootsie/Anger

Tootsie never made it home in time for Sunday dinner. Just as she stood up from the pew to leave, she saw him. He gently mouthed her name, and her breath caught in her throat. She hoped she didn't appear too anxious. After all, it wasn't every day that a full-blooded, thick-neck man remembered her name. She calmed herself by counting to ten as Adonis made his way toward her. *Breathe.*

She was pleased to see that the twinkle in his eyes matched her own, though it threatened to cut her air supply in two. Tootsie's cheeks warmed. What was he saying? *Focus, Tootsie.* Adonis's voice seduced her ears into playing deaf. She missed what he said.

He stared into her eyes, waiting for a response.

"Uh-huh." She felt stupid.

"Good. My car's parked right outside. Let's go."

What had he just asked? What was she getting herself into?

"Lead the way." She grinned, excited by her own boldness.

"No, after you," he insisted, watching her gaze lower.

Tootsie didn't care that the dry cleaners had shrunk her black suit—again—or that her big toes were poking through her stockings. As long as her hair was right, she was tight. Too short a 'do didn't exist in her scissor-happy stylist's book. Since Tootsie was rockin' a fresh cut, it was all good.

A couple of her church sisters turned to watch them go. Tootsie slowed her stroll, enjoying every bit of attention. Leaving the church with an attractive man on her heels upped her stock, making her feel like the most coveted woman in town. Adonis was popping all kinds of cherries. Better guard the master one, she reminded herself.

Once outside, Adonis led Tootsie to his navy blue Hyundai. The front bucket seat was a tight fit, but she managed to squeeze all of her body parts in before he closed the door. She came this close to calling her best friend Bubbles while he made his way around the front of the car. Instead, she let out the passenger seat as he slid behind the wheel.

Tootsie had a momentary flash of fear. She didn't know this man from Adam. If he chopped her up into a million pieces and threw her remains into the next dumpster, who would know? Better squeeze in a quick text to Bubbles. As she fumbled in her purse for the phone, though, the sudden heat from his hand on her knee banished all other thoughts, overruling her intention.

Tootsie stole a head-to-toe shot of Adonis as he turned the ignition. She couldn't escape his aftershave. Tingling, she clamped her thighs shut. Smiling, she turned away, hiding her grin behind her hand.

"Comfortable?" he asked, driving off.

"Very." She eased back into the black leather cocoon, her head squeaking against the headrest.

"Good."

Tootsie glimpsed his dimple. Was it really all for her? His bad-boy swagger was already taking her mind places it needn't be, and he wasn't bad-looking until he opened wide. She was itching to whip out one of her dental hygiene tools and get busy in his mouth. Her brand-new scaler would do the trick. Her musing was interrupted by another whiff of aftershave. Heaven help them both if he got any closer to her.

"I know this great little spot in Cambria Heights." Adonis kept his eyes on the road. "They serve the best jazz brunch in town."

"Okay."

They drove a few minutes in silence, while Tootsie tried to figure out what attracted him to her. She kept it real. She wasn't exactly New York's finest, so why her?

With one eye on the road, Adonis hit Sirius. Smiling, Tootsie closed her eyes as the music engulfed them. She said a quick prayer. *Lord, let him be the one. Let him be the one.* As she opened her eyes, they pulled up to the restaurant. Adonis reached for Tootsie's hand, kissing it gently. Another cherry . . . popped.

By the time Tootsie arrived home Sunday night, the ten o'clock news was half over. She unlocked the door and tiptoed inside. The living room was shrouded in darkness. Relieved, she let out a sigh and hugged herself tightly. That's when the timer turned on nearly every damn light in the house. Lilly appeared, sitting with arms crossed in the recliner. Tootsie allowed her arms to fall back down to her sides as her smile evaporated.

"Where were you, daughter?" Lilly asked.

"Just out." Tootsie couldn't meet her gaze.

"Didn't I tell you to be home in time for dinner?"

"Yes."

"And? Which part of that didn't you understand?" Lilly continued. "Do I ask a lot from you?"

"No." Tootsie sighed. *Here it comes. Again.*

"Then would it hurt you to have Sunday dinner with your poor old mother, huh?"

"Of course not."

"Good. Now, where were you?"

"With Bubbles." She made a mental note to secure her alibi.

Lilly gave her daughter a sleepy side eye. "Bubbles? You've been with Bubbles all day? I don't care if she is the deacon's wife. She's bad news. Her fake lashes are so heavy, I don't know where she gets the strength to blink. I know the family, remember? And who names their daughter Bubbles, anyway?"

"Who names their child Tootsie?" she shot back at Lilly.

"That's not your government name. It's just a nickname. There's a difference. Her and her sisters are nothing but a bunch of whores, every last one of them. The mama was a slut before she could walk, and they say the grandmother turned tricks in her diapers."

"Mama," Tootsie exclaimed.

"The apple don't fall far from the tree, is all I'm saying. Remember that, daughter. She'll have your name in lights."

"So, tell me about him," Bubbles insisted over Dunkin' Donuts a few days later.

Tootsie closed her eyes and smiled. "Adonis has dimples for days, a little rough around the edges, and a thick neck," she said slowly for emphasis.

The deacon's wife lowered her voice. "Lord knows I miss those thugs and their thick . . . necks. Just be careful out here in these streets."

Tootsie had promised herself that the second she turned legal, she'd move out of her mother's house and free herself from Lilly's clutches. That was seventeen years ago, and her bags were still half-packed and hidden underneath her bed. It wasn't easy being the daughter of Missionary Lilly White, nor being the only thirty-five-year-old virgin in town. She tried to ignore the jokes about her mother, claiming she was as sanctified as a praying mantis, or that underneath her long skirts she peed standing up, but her fists hadn't let her. She came home from school many a day looking like a wild child, her clothes torn, snot drooling down her chin. Her mother was a good woman—when she wasn't shredding her nerves. Like her insistence that Tootsie keep her "V account" closed until marriage. Fine advice for a teenager. But her clock was ticking, and Tootsie wasn't trying to be no modern-day Sarah, pushing old age and still childless.

One time, she had vented her frustrations to her mother.

"I know how you feel, daughter," Lilly had told her. "Just keep the faith. Your day'll come. In times like these, draw upon your faith. Ask God to give you strength."

"Maybe I'll schedule a session with Pastor Dante." Tootsie knew her mother couldn't stand him, but Tootsie thought he was thank-you-Jesus fine.

"I'm your mother. I gave you life. What can he do?'"

"Guess you're right," Tootsie agreed, but she met with Pastor Dante the following week. If Missionary Collins hadn't been hovering all during the meeting, things would have been cool.

"Ignore her," Pastor Dante had told Tootsie. "Now, what's on your mind?"

Tootsie took a deep breath. Damn that old heifer listening in on their conversation. "Pastor Dante, I am thirty-five years old with no husband in sight. I don't know what to do."

"Sister Tootsie, focus on your first love. God's time is not always our time. Sometimes, instead of concentrating on what we don't have, we need to praise God for what we do have. It's not easy, but be patient."

"I am being patient, but—"

"Sister Tootsie, your but is too big."

She shifted uncomfortably in her chair. "Excuse me?"

"Your b-u-t," he explained.

"Oh, okay."

He continued. "Sister Tootsie, have you been reading your Bible? Do you make time for God?"

"Absolutely." She managed a smile.

"How often?"

"Not as often as I should, but when I'm pressed for time, I listen to the CD. You know, the one narrated by Blair Underwear?"

"Help me, Jesus," Missionary Collins grabbed her heart with one hand and the bookcase with the other.

Take me now, Lord. Just take me now.

Tootsie's alarm went off much too soon. The thought of going to work put her right back to sleep. Ten minutes turned into twenty. Now she knew she had to get up. She lay there for a few more minutes, prepping for eight hours of hell. Before she knew it, she was half an hour late. Working interfered with her life. Still, she did the math and planted both feet firmly on the floor. *Adam and Eve, you did this to me.*

Being a dental hygienist was like pulling teeth, only worse. Most patients came less than once a year, but blamed her for the torture they said she inflicted. If they brought their behinds in more often, she wouldn't have to work so hard. She wanted to open up their heads and shoot some sense into them. Then again, their ignorance provided the perfect outlet for her aggression.

Tootsie walked in late like it was early. The morning crawled along, and as usual, she lunched past the hour. Adonis's late afternoon text changed everything.

She saw eleven patients that day, being extra gentle to ten of them, but that last patient caught it. Tootsie checked the clock above the sink as she placed the saliva ejector in her patient's mouth. She'd have to do a rush job. Tootsie donned her goggles and began cleaning, drowning out the patient's cries each time one of the smooth, metallic scalers hit a nerve.

Tootsie barely had a chance to remove her smock and sign out before racing out the door. She ran three lights before she got jammed up in traffic. Instinctively, she reached for a cigarette, then stopped, popping a pill for her high blood pressure instead. She didn't want to smell like dirty butts for Adonis.

Thank goodness Lilly was holed up in her room, her television blasting as usual. Tootsie might as well have had the house to herself. She turned on the shower and lathered up, so much so that if she hadn't grabbed the handrail, she would have slid and busted her behind as she stepped out. She draped a large bath sheet around her bodacious self and headed back to the bedroom.

She lotioned down, perfumed up, and ran a brush through her hair. Finally, she applied a touch of makeup and lipstick, reaching for a wet, gooey gloss to top it off. Bubbles' words of wisdom echoed: *Honey, the only wet and sticky lips that'll drive a man nuts are between your legs.* Tootsie ditched the gloss.

She slipped on her favorite bra, loving the way it made mountains out of her molehills, but the matching thong dug into her like dental floss. She squeezed into outfit number one, eyed her mirror, and shuddered. She could hear the fashion police picking apart the white cigarette pants and peplum top that only maxed out her width. Better go with choice number two, a cap-sleeved baby blue sheath that cried casual sophistication—with the right undergarments. Where the hell were her Spanx? She took three minutes to locate them and another ten minutes to squeeze into them. She'd need the jaws of life to break free, but hey . . .

Tight and ripe, a Spanxed-down Tootsie paused and looked around as she entered the dimly lit lounge an hour later. Spotting him in the shadows, she smiled as his eyes drew her into the seat next to his.

"Look great." He grinned as he took his eye off the big screen for a sec and checked his phone. "Our table'll be ready in a few."

Tootsie popped a few peanuts in her mouth to quiet the growling, praying that peanut gook wasn't forming between her teeth as she talked. She nursed a wine spritzer while Adonis downed a whiskey with a side of club soda.

"Two drinks?" she asked him, confused.

"Separation of church and state," he informed her.

Tootsie threw back her head and laughed.

Oh, she ready.

Chapter 7

Sable/Greed

Sable craved a long, hot soak. A day of housecleaning, grocery shopping, and running errands had taken its toll. She began stripping off her clothes en route to the bedroom, where she selected a pair of lime green silk pajamas for after her bubble bath. Sable added her favorite bath gel, lit a few candles, and eased herself into the scented water.

Sable's thoughts drifted back to Sunday's service—and to Pastor Dante. Lately, she had been thinking about him more than she ought. She had told him how much she had enjoyed the morning message as he greeted the congregation after service.

"Thank you," he said, giving her a quick hug. "Love the dress," he added sotto voce before releasing her. She rarely wore sundresses to church, but the day was a scorcher.

"Pastor Dante, I need to have a word with you," Missionary White barked from a few yards away, breaking the spell.

Sable rushed to her car, anxious to be alone with her thoughts. She didn't want to read anything into her pastor's comment, but she knew what she knew. The tension was building. Sable couldn't get home fast enough, and the tingling between her legs rose unbearably as she came to a screeching halt at a stoplight. By the time she pulled into the garage, her clinging panties reminded her just who was boss.

Price was precisely where she had left him earlier that morning—on the sofa, his eyes glued to a tennis match. She had removed her dress and stood in front of the TV, blocking his view. Next, she untied her hair, letting it fall long and free. Facing him, Sable slid onto his lap, already aware of Price's erection. He kissed her hard before unhooking her bra and succumbing to her allure.

"Shoot, I forgot to stop and get bread," Sable blurted out.

He tugged at her panties and unzipped his pants. "Don't worry, baby, I got your loaf."

"Ooh, whole wheat?" she moaned.

"You know it." He thrust deep inside her.

Sable passionately kissed her husband, or was she kissing the pastor? The two faces blurred into one. Wrapping her arms around his neck, Sable held on tight. She imagined herself touching, tasting, feeling him within until her body quivered, breaking out in spasms.

"Is it mine, baby?" Price whispered in her ear as she came.

Sable closed her eyes. "All of it."

Running errands later that week, Sable never expected to be breaking bread with her pastor, but she had stopped at Tango Mango for a fruit salad on the way home, and there he was. Grinning, he picked up on their mutual vibe and approached her table.

"May I join you?" he asked before sitting.

"Of course." She smiled as he pulled up a chair opposite her.

"Wow, orange really looks good on you."

"Thank you, Pastor."

"Call me David. Time out for formalities. Don't you think?"

"Mmm . . . I'd rather not—out of respect for my first lady," she told him.

"Your first lady," he repeated, taking a sip of his smoothie before leaning forward.

"That is correct." She curled a loose strand of hair around her ear with one hand while tossing the salad with the other.

"Okay, and not out of respect for your husband? We'll get back to your first lady in a minute."

Sable stuttered ever so slightly. "I–I . . . just want to keep it respectful."

"So, you think calling me by my first name would somehow . . . What? Help me out here," he teased.

"It's just . . . easier . . . for both of us. For all of us."

"You love your husband?"

"Yes." She slid a forkful of salad into her mouth and chewed slowly.

"And I take it that you're in love with him too."

"Very much so," she agreed.

"And he feels the same for you." He said it more as a statement than a question. "That's beautiful . . . and rare. You two are truly blessed because marriages aren't always what they seem."

"Something tells me this is where First Lady comes in." Pushing the line, Sable dipped her sweet, manicured toe where it didn't belong, and she was learning that it didn't take much to stir her pastor's pot. Sable put down her fork and waited.

"I couldn't ask for a more perfect first lady, but can I be blunt?" he asked before proceeding. "She's too saved and sanctified for my bed."

Sable sank back in her seat, beyond stunned. "But you guys seem like the perfect couple, like you're so much in love. So much affection."

"What we *are* are two incredible actors playing incredible roles and following the script."

Sable shook her head in disbelief. "I had no idea. How long has it been?"

"Six months."

"Does the punishment fit the crime? Wives don't go on strike for nothing. You must've done something," she insisted.

"She was all over me when we were dating. I hung onto abstinence for dear life. Chantel drove me nuts. We did everything but—Half the time I could barely take Communion."

"And now?" Sable pressed.

"Nothing."

"And how long have you been married?"

"Six. Months." He enunciated both syllables.

"Hold up. So your marriage was never consummated?" She frowned.

"My wife is a master manipulator. In bed, in the shower, the game is always the same. Look, but don't touch. I'm tired of her games. All we do is play games."

"Maybe you're unequally yoked. Do you think she's gay?" Sable pried.

"No, I think I remind her of someone from her past. Ever hear that old expression—excuse me, Sable—family fucks you first? Maybe we both moved too fast, and our marriage triggers each other's demons and unhealed childhood wounds."

Sable took a breath. "That's deep. Do you still love her?"

"Do I still love her?" He thought for a moment. "I take my marriage vows seriously, too, but I'm a man. I have needs, and she's setting me up to fail. It's hard sometimes.

But to answer your question, despite the cat-and-mouse games, yeah, I still love my wife."

"I'm sure she's feeling the heat, too."

"Are you speaking from experience?" he asked.

"Sometimes." Sable exhaled. "There are nights my unanswered calls go straight to voicemail, and that's not a position a wise man should want his wife to be in. Neglect is dangerous. It can make you feel . . ." She paused, searching for the right word.

"Restless," he suggested.

"Yes." She couldn't meet his gaze. "So," she continued, "I've been begging God not to allow me to do anything foolish like breaking my wedding vows."

"You've never been unfaithful?"

"No, I haven't," she said, shaking her head.

As if taking time out for a moment of prayer, Pastor Dante closed his eyes and then opened them before speaking. "Neither have I."

Sable stopped to pick up a few things at the supermarket, her pastor's revelation still fresh in her mind. She placed the items on the conveyor belt as the lady ahead of her was just wrapping up. Stocked with baby food and diapers, the lady peeled off bills to the cashier, but she was several dollars short. A customer at the next station turned around and offered to pay the balance. The young mother refused, appearing embarrassed by the offer. Sable found a twenty-dollar bill in her pocket and allowed it to fall to the floor by the young mother's feet.

Motioning to the young mother, Sable asked. "Is that your twenty down there?"

She glanced at her feet and eagerly scooped up the bill. "Thank you." She peered into Sable's eyes and smiled. "Thank you so much."

"You're welcome," Sable told her simply. "Don't forget your change."

She accepted the change and the receipt from the cashier and smiled. "Take care. God bless," she added.

"God bless you too," Sable reminded her.

Chapter 8

Pastor Dante sat at a table for two in the nearly empty diner. His lips were wrapped around a perfect cup of scalding hot coffee as he decompressed from a busy morning. His client's wife hadn't liked any of the designs David had created for their new home. He had a lot on his mind, and the diner's peace proved a blessing.

Sable walked in just as he ordered a second cup. She was deep in thought and didn't notice him. He dared not interrupt. After several sips, he signaled for the waitress and paid his bill, catching Sable's eye on the way out. Her smile lured him over to her side.

"Pastor Dante." She perked up. "You weren't going to leave without saying hello, were you?"

His eyes never left hers. "Absolutely not. I just didn't want to intrude."

"You, an intrusion?" Sable stroked her long, sleek ponytail as it rested on her right shoulder, its layers embracing her breast. She seemed to enjoy the power she had over him. He was under her spell, and she knew it. "Wanna join me?"

Pastor Dante slid into the booth opposite her. He checked his watch. "I have some time between appointments."

"Lucky me," she confessed.

He shot her a look.

"I didn't mean it like that," she admitted.

"So, how exactly did you mean it?"

"Funny, I am so warm all of a sudden." Sable quickly freed her ponytail and gathered it in a French twist. She reached inside her purse for a hair clip.

"Better?" he asked.

"Much."

"Yeah, it's definitely heating up outside. Another scorcher."

A waitress appeared to take her order. "Hi, I'm Erin. Are you ready to order?"

"Just coffee," Sable replied.

"And you, sir?"

"No, I'm fine," he told her. "Thank you."

Erin promptly returned with Sable's coffee. Sable reached for the milk and sugar, slowly stirring them into her coffee. She took a sip and smiled in appreciation.

"I'm really glad I ran into you today, Sister Sable," Pastor Dante began. "God answers prayers."

"That He does."

The flirtation had gone on long enough. "I need to apologize," he said.

"For what?" she asked, an eleven forming between her brows.

"For saying anything you may have perceived as inappropriate behavior. We are both married, and if I've stepped out of line in any way, if I've said anything unbecoming a pastor—or for that matter, a married man—I'm sorry." As if in prayer, Sable shielded her eyes from view with her hand for a moment and then took a deep breath. She wrapped a stray strand of hair behind her ear before meeting his gaze.

"I owe you an apology, too."

This time, he was the one caught off guard. "Why do you think you owe me an apology?"

"Because, Pastor Dante, I am just as married as you are, and I have no business entertaining the kind of thoughts I've been having about you."

He kept his cool, though he hardly felt that way. "I'm sure it was all innocent."

"Flirting between a man and a woman is rarely harmless and never innocent."

"So, what kinds of thoughts have you been entertaining?" he said, nervously playing with a packet of sweetener.

"I think we both know the answer to that."

"I want to hear you say it."

"David, I—I . . ." she stammered.

"I've been waiting so long just to hear you say my name. Now, tell me what you want me to do to you."

"I . . . I can't do this." Sable stood and rushed out the door.

"Sable, wait."

She had left her credit card.

David called her the next day from church. "I have your credit card. Come and get it."

"What time will you—"

He hung up.

She drove to the church and walked inside to the vestibule. "Stop looking at me like that," she whispered as he escorted her straight into his office.

"How long, Sable?" David asked.

"How long what?"

"How long do we have to play these games? I don't know how much longer I can last."

Sable shook her head. "I don't know what you're talking—"

"Stop it." He silenced her gently. "I'm a grown man. Don't play with me, Sable, okay? You know exactly what I'm talking about. Let's be clear. We've danced around this long enough. We're not in high school. You no longer have the luxury of playing shy or innocent or hard to get or whatever else you women want to call it, not after all the cold showers and sleepless nights you've put me through. You don't have that right. You know exactly what I'm talking about, and I know exactly what you're doing. You think that as long as your fantasies stay discreetly tucked away in your mind, they don't exist? That as long as we don't talk about them, we're safe?"

"What do you want from me?" she asked.

A knock at the door only delayed the inevitable. Deacon Greer peeked in, and his eyes popped open at the sight of Sable. "Sorry, Pastor, I didn't mean to interrupt. I thought you were alone."

"That's quite all right, Deac."

"Praise the Lord, Sister Sable."

"Good to see you, Deacon."

"How's Brother Galore?" Deacon Greer asked.

She wasn't missing all the subtle undertones. "He's fine." She smiled. "Thank you for asking."

"Please give him my regards," he added.

"I certainly shall." She nodded.

"Pastor Dante, the plumber Missionary Collins called is here about the leak, and she wants to see you in the kitchen."

"Thanks, Deac. Please tell her I'll be right there."

"Sure, Pastor."

Pastor Dante waited until Deacon Greer closed the door and his footsteps echoed faintly in the distance. He stood. "This isn't over," he told her, "but our church hugs are."

Chapter 9

One Saturday a month, Sable volunteered at the church's soup kitchen as part of her personal ministry. But as the sexual tension between her and the pastor grew, she was tempted to stay home.

Dressed for comfort in a navy sweatsuit and sneakers and modest jewelry, Sable entered One Way's side entrance and proceeded to the lower sanctuary. She joined the other women in a corporate prayer before they busied themselves in the kitchen. Baked chicken, fried chicken, lasagna, green beans, mashed potatoes, and garden salad were just a few of the items on the menu for the lunchtime crowd—not to mention an assortment of fresh fruit, cakes, pies, and gelatin. They spruced up the church's basement with balloons, tablecloths, and matching plates, napkins, and utensils.

Noon arrived before they knew it, and they opened up the doors of the church. Pastor Dante blessed the food and made the rounds, spending a moment welcoming each guest, visitor, and neighbor, inviting them to return on Sunday morning for worship.

The usual homeless man with the scar was there that day. Joined to a small raggedy shopping cart, he wore blue jeans and a cotton long-sleeve shirt. He was always clean, his eyes—all pupil. Sable never knew the deaf mute's name, but when she piled his plate high, his toothless grin spoke volumes.

For some reason, her spirit connected with him. She always prepared a special care package just for him, filled with new clothing and undergarments that she purchased herself. Sable also included a generous supply of soap, toothpaste, deodorant, lotion, toothbrushes, tissue, and washcloths to last the entire month. She even included a variety of snacks, such as chips, nuts, mints, chewing gum, candy, and plenty of bottled water. Every human on the planet deserved to be clean and feel good about themselves, whether they had an address or not.

Sable still remembered the first time their paths had crossed. She had driven into the city that morning and ended up taking the railroad home when her old car died. The E train had just left the Jamaica–Van Wyck subway station on its way to Sutphin Boulevard. A homeless man sitting across the way motioned for the bottled water in her hand. She brushed him off, but not before she caught wind of a nightmarish scar across his forehead. She had never seen such a hideously gruesome sight. It nearly occupied his entire forehead from above the eyebrows to just below his hairline. She couldn't figure out how someone could possibly get a scar like that and live to tell about it. All she knew was that she had to be on the next train to Baldwin Hills in less than five minutes because she had to be home, relaxed and ready for three full hours of fantasy gold jewelry. Just the thought of missing out on all that jewelry was a sin.

The homeless man squeezed his neck while eyeing her bottle of water. Suddenly, Sable felt shame. The Bible was full of references to the living water, and here she had just denied a homeless man something she should have given him freely. Nana Jones had taught her to be careful of how she treated strangers because she could be entertaining angels unaware.

Sable tried to get the homeless man's attention again. She transferred the bottle of water from her right hand to her left, hoping the movement would catch his eye. It didn't. He was too busy checking out a man with a nervous twitch.

Oh, please give me another chance. Please, God, just one more chance. I'm sorry. Let him look at me again.

After what seemed like an eternity, the homeless man looked her way. Sable leaned forward, offering him the water. He quickly snatched it out of her hand, popped the top, and guzzled it down. *Thank you, Jesus.* Sable prayed as she exited the E. As she prepared to board the Long Island Railroad to Baldwin Hills, she caught a glimpse of the clock. It was seven eleven. She felt redeemed. Nana Jones would be pleased.

Sable smiled as Alejandra Katz approached the buffet. She had become a regular at the soup kitchen ever since Sable dropped her a twenty that day in the supermarket. Her three kids ran over to Sable while she walked across the room to get more plastic plates. Five-year-old Maya tugged at Sable's sleeve.

"I like your T," she told Sable, admiring her gold necklace.

"You like my cross?" Sable smiled at her innocence.

"Uh-huh."

"Well, you're just as sweet as a little love bug." Sable gave them each a hug before returning to the serving station.

The line was halfway out the door and growing larger by the moment. By this time, Sable's feet ached from standing on the painted cement floor. Her sneakers' padded insoles took up some of the slack—but not all of it. Lunch lasted for another four hours before dessert was served. The cakes and pies went like they were caught up in the rapture. Luckily, they had made enough for all those who wanted.

Sable managed to save extra meals for Alejandra and her kids. She wrapped up the extra meals and stopped by Alejandra's table to chat. She sank down into the chair, gazing down at her swollen ankles.

"You must be exhausted," Alejandra told her.

"Exhausted isn't the word," Sable agreed. "But it's for a good cause."

"You have a kind heart. That's why you're so blessed. I think I'll go home and have a glass of wine. These kids are wearing me out."

"And growing like little weeds."

"I know." She laughed before her smile disappeared. "Nicholas, if you don't turn around and eat your food," she warned her middle child. "Sable, they don't give me a moment's rest. Sometimes I feel like pulling my hair out. You'll see. Want some practice?"

"One day." Sable grinned. "So, how's life treating you?"

"No use complaining." Alejandra shrugged. "Gotta stay positive for my crew here. Right, guys?"

The children were in their own world, enjoying every bit of chocolate cake they could cram down their tiny throats.

Alejandra continued. "I have a job interview next week."

"Let me know if you need any references," Sable told her.

"Really?"

"Girl, you know I got you. Just give me a call."

"Thanks, Sable. Means a lot."

Sable lay back on the sofa with her feet in Price's lap, enjoying her foot massage. She moaned. "Ooh, that feels good."

"What's going on, Sable?"

"What do you mean?"

"Normally, you come home from church upbeat, but lately, you haven't been yourself. You seem . . . preoccupied. Talk to me."

"I don't know. Guess I need a vacation. You ready for Montego Bay?"

"Am I ready? Is water wet? Let me get rid of some things on my calendar at work, and I'm all yours."

"Promise?"

"Promise."

Chapter 10

David tossed and turned. His wife still wouldn't let him touch her. How many more cold showers and lonely nights lay ahead? How long would his marriage survive—if he could even call it a marriage? His thoughts drifted to Sable. The more he saw her, the more he wanted her. He couldn't shake her from his mind. How often did she make love to her husband? Did he satisfy her in bed? Yes, he was a pastor, but at the end of the day, his flesh struggled with temptation like everyone else's. How long could he fight the good fight? How long could he keep up this façade of having it all together while lust slowly devoured his foundation?

Price ran into David at the gas station and confronted him as they both pumped. "What the hell is going on between you and my wife? Lately, every time she comes home from church, she's . . . different. And I see the way you look at her."

"No different from the way you been looking at mine," David shot back.

"Well, at least I have the balls to do something about it. Here."

"What's this? Option number one. A blank check for one night with your wife."

At first there was nothing between them but silence. He shook his head. "Is this a joke?"

"No." Price slipped the blank check in David's shirt pocket. "Think it over and give me a call me when you're ready, or we can go with option number two and open things up."

"What are you saying?"

"You know exactly what I'm saying."

"Yeah, well, there's some itches only God should scratch, okay? Look, I'm a pastor and I'm not down for that."

"Look, I don't know what's going on or not going on between you and your wife, but lemme tell you something about lust, Pastor. When it hits, it hits hard. Think about your ministry. Your legacy. If you don't get this under control, it's gonna tear up your church and eat you alive."

"Nah, I'm good." David shut it down quickly.

"Are you?" Price shook his head as he hopped in his car and drove off.

Two weeks later Price's words hit like a brick. Struggling to prepare Sunday's message, David went for a late-night drive. With a hard-on bigger than the law should allow, he pulled into an abandoned lot and reclined, imagining the taste of Sable on his tongue. Unable to contain himself, he loosened his shirt and pants, thankful for tinted windows. He closed his eyes and found refuge in the fleeting warmth between her thighs and drifted off. He jumped as a police cruiser pulled up behind him, and an officer stepped out of the vehicle.

David returned his seat to the upright position and quickly grabbed a book from the glove compartment to hide his erection, his shirt still untucked. He rolled down the window.

"Pastor Dante?" The officer shone a flashlight into David's passenger seat and rear. "What you reading?"

David looked down. "Bible," he said under his breath, his gaze forward.

The officer shook his head, his eyes sick with disappointment. "You know something? My wife attends your church. Matter of fact, she's always singing your praises. I could give you a fine, but I'ma let you go." He headed to his cruiser, shaking his head, and then turned back to David. "Oh, and Sunday's message better be *fiyah*."

David zipped up and drove off, heart pumping through the roof. Price's words tailgated all the way home.

"We need to talk." Less than a week later, David and Price broke bread at the Mango Tango off the Southern State Parkway.

"Heard about your run-in with the law the other day," Price told him over green juice.

"I felt like a doggone teenager. Talk about embarrassing."

"Man, you better be glad his wife is one of my best customers. Know what I'm saying?"

"Thanks, man. I just thought I had it together."

"We always have it together until we don't. I don't know why you're being so hard on yourself. For whatever reason, you're a man whose needs aren't being met. So, before you destroy your church, you need to handle your business."

"My wife would never—"

"You'd be surprised."

With Price's indecent proposal and sweat oozing from every pore, David fought to reach the next level on the Peloton. Could he really pull this off? Could he go through with this and still call himself a man of God?

Could he talk Chantel into being down with it too? It would definitely be a hard sell. *Lord knows I'm already going to hell. Might as well book a first class.*

Chantel popped her head in the doorway and told David that breakfast was almost ready. He finished up in the shower just as Chantel fixed their plates. After a quick grace, they dug in.

"Ooh, this is good." He cut into the perfectly seasoned egg white omelet.

"You're in a good mood." She smiled and brought the mug to her lips.

"I don't know what I'd do without you."

"Wow, where'd that come from?"

"We need to talk."

"Okay." She gave him her full attention. "What's up?"

"Look, I can't go on like this. We can't go on like this. I need you in my bed. I didn't sign up for this."

"You're right. You do. But . . ." She paused. "I can't give you what's not in me to give, and divorce was never an option, remember?"

"As your husband, you trust me?"

"I do." She softened. "And I never intended for our marriage to go left. I mean, not this left. You gotta believe me, David."

"I do." He reached for her hand and gave a reassuring squeeze. "There's something I need to tell you. I got pulled over by the cops the other day."

She pulled her hand out of his and exclaimed, "Oh my God! What happened?"

"I was parked in an abandoned lot. I started masturbating, and a cop pulled up behind me."

"How could you be so careless? David, if this gets out, our ministry is ruined, and we're done."

"Here's the thing. The cop's wife goes to our church. She's a big supporter of our ministry, and she's a big client of Sister Sable's husband." David took a deep breath as he prepared to get a little reckless with the truth. "Anyway, I spoke to Sable's husband, and he thinks he can talk the cop into making it all go away. He wants to meet us for dinner to brainstorm. You in?"

"Oh, I'm all in."

The four of them met at a hot new lounge off the Rockaway Turnpike. Over dinner and drinks, they set up their rules of engagement.

"For this to work, I think we need some ground rules," Price began, cutting into his salmon. David nodded while taking a bite of lamb.

"For starters, I think we can all agree that what happens between us stays between us." David looked at his wife, Price, and Sable.

"Ya think we should have a designated schedule?" Chantel asked the others.

"Uh-uh. Let's keep it hot and spicy, but we should always use protection." Sable took a sip of wine before putting the glass down. "No exceptions."

"Girl, that's a good one. And I think we should always be under the same roof. No private hook-ups. Too much is at stake." Chantel reached for her napkin and wiped her mouth.

"Look, all I ask is that we leave our inhibitions at the door and have some fun." Price laughed, and they all joined in as he threw back his second drink.

David asked, "Everybody down?"

They all looked at each other before nodding in agreement.

"Okay. Tomorrow night. Let's do this!"

David was so excited he could barely sleep. He woke up the next morning to his wife in tears.

"I can't . . . I can't do this. I'm sorry, David. I just can't."
She started to hyperventilate. "I . . . I . . . I ca . . . I ca."

"It's okay. It's okay. Breathe. Breathe."

"You're disappointed. Aren't you?"

"I'm not. It's okay. We'll get through this."

"You promise? All this time I've been such an ass. Let's try and make it work."

He kissed her on the forehead. "Go back to sleep. Get some rest. I'll make you some herbal tea."

"Thanks," she said simply, reaching for a tissue and blowing her nose.

David closed the bedroom door and headed for the kitchen. He called Price and heard the anticipation in his voice

"Are you guys as excited as we are? Man, we barely slept a wink last night. Felt like kids on Christmas Eve up in here."

"Nah, Price, Chantel changed her mind. She's not ready. She's just not ready," David repeated.

"Whaddaya mean? She seemed so down last night."

"That's Chantel for you."

"Well, you hang in there," Price told him. "It ain't over."

Price turned up the air conditioning and got back under the covers with Sable. She snuggled against his chest.

"Please don't tell me what I think you're about to tell me."

"You guessed it." He shrugged. "She chickened out."

"She probably just got cold feet. Tell David I'll talk to her. You know I'm persuasive." She grinned as he rolled her over onto her back.

"Yes, you are, sweetheart." He kissed her neck. "Yes, you are."

***

It poured the day Sable and Chantel met for lunch at the Seafood Plaza out in Hempstead, but neither wanted to cancel. They checked their raincoats and umbrellas and were promptly seated because the restaurant was practically empty.

"You look radiant," Chantel commented after the waiter took their orders and left them alone.

"Thank you." Sable smiled as she sipped her coconut water. "My husband does have his way. Best masseuse ever."

"When's the last time you've had a good one?"

Chantel rolled her eyes. "Oh, my goodness."

"That long? I bet David gives great massages. Why are you depriving yourself?"

"That's a story for another day, but you could be glowing too if you played your cards right."

As if on cue, the server returned with their piping hot salmon, black beans and rice, and steamed vegetables. "Muy caliente," he warned before walking away.

Chantel said grace, and they dug in. "Ooh, this is good," she said as she enjoyed her first bite.

"Mm-hmm," Sable agreed, nodding slowly. "Like I said, why deprive yourself the simple pleasures in life? Only you can answer that. But in the meantime, if you and your husband are suffering, then somthing needs to give. How long do you think you can keep the charade up? Eventually, we all need some kind of release. Know what I mean?"

"Of course."

"Just think about. Give it some more thought. No pressure. That's all," she said gently.

***

David called and finally gave Price the news he'd been hoping for. Now, they could proceed with their plan.

"Morning, beautiful." Price kissed Sable gently on the cheek. She rubbed her eyes, stirring.

"You're dressed. I musta overslept. What time is it?" She stretched and yawned. "Lemme fix you breakfast." She sat up.

"I'll grab something on the way in. No worries. Besides, I have a surprise for you."

"Ooh, I like surprises."

"Not you?" He laughed and kissed the tip of her nose before adjusting his tie. "Well, you're gonna love this one. I've been so busy lately. I wanna make it up to you. I want you to go shopping, get your hair and nails done, get that massage, makeup, the works."

"Say no more."

"Put it on my Black card. I want you relaxed and sexy AF."

"What's going on? Must be big."

"Huge. I'll text you the deets later. Can you be ready by say . . . eight?"

"You're the boss."

He chuckled. "Yeah, I am, ain't I?" He kissed her hand and stood. "Call you later."

Sable sank back into the pillow and kicked her heels, grinning until her cheeks hurt. What a way to start the day! She jumped up and made the appointments, treating herself to the works.

Later that afternoon, Sable received a text from Price. **Meet me at the Marriott. Room 1408 9pm.**

Looking forward to a spicy night with her husband, she took one last look at her voluptuousness and headed out the door. Traffic was light, and she arrived in no time. She checked in with the front desk and headed up to the room.

"Damn, you look hot." Price admired her curves from every angle. "Com'ere, girl." He took her in his arms. "You hungry?"

"Let's order in," she suggested

"As good as you look? Nah, we goin' downstairs. Lemme grab my sports jacket."

Holding hands, they exited the elevator and ran into David and Chantel.

"What's up?" Price asked as he and Sable rounded a corner. "We're headed to the restaurant for dinner. Why don't you join us? It'll be fun. Right, babe?" he asked Sable.

"Absolutely," she agreed.

"Okay, let's do this." David grinned.

They entered the restaurant and were seated shortly thereafter. After appetizers, entrees, and two bottles of wine, David and Price suggested that the wives return to their rooms while they tweaked some business ideas. Sable rubbed her ankle and stood, eager to ditch her stilettos.

"Slip into something sexy. I won't be long." Price wrapped his arms around Sable's waist and grinned up at her. Chantel's eyes quickly darted away as she said her good-nights, too.

Startled, Chantel jumped out of bed. "Price? How'd you get in here?" She watched as he removed his jacket without saying a word.

"David and I swapped keys. He's down the hall with Sable." He unbuttoned his shirt.

"So, tonight's the night?"

"You ask too many questions. That day you caught me at the light? This right here is what you wanted." He unzipped his fly. "Com'ere."

"Exactly what I wanted," she finally admitted, helping him remove his dress shirt.

Price untied her robe. He wrapped his arms inside and grabbed a handful of her nakedness before sliding his tongue into her mouth.

An hour later and still no Price, Sable hopped in the shower and lathered up. She smiled as he pulled up behind her and milked her breasts. Relishing his touch, Sable closed her eyes and then turned to kiss his lips under the stream of wetness.

"Hey, babe."

She opened her eyes and jumped back. "David! How'd you . . . Where's Price?" She flung her wet hair to one side.

"Down the hall with Chantel."

This is wild." Suddenly, she laughed.

"And long overdue. Your husband adores you, Sable, and he knows you're in good hands. You don't have to choose. You can have us both."

She wrapped her arms around his neck as their tongues dove in, deeply, hungrily. Finally, they came up for air.

"I couldn't take it anymore, Sable. I had to have you."

"Neither could I, David. I had to have you, too. And Chantel's finally down for this?" She searched his eyes, cupping his face.

"Your husband is boning my wife as we speak," he assured her.

He backed her up and pinned her against the glass shower wall. She wrapped her legs around his waist, totally open, totally ready. He penetrated her warmth as she held onto his neck. Not a drop of daylight between them as the water glided off their backs.

Enjoying the hypnotic friction between them, Sable moaned as her eyes rolled backward and her body broke out into spasms of deliciousness. Grunting and groaning, David grabbed her by the nape of her neck as he exploded inside of her, his essence running down her thigh until he was completely emptied.

Panting, Sable dismounted while David leaned back against the glass for support. After he took a moment to catch his breath, David pulled her back in and slid his tongue into her mouth, slowly caressing her sweetness. Then, he swooped her up in his arms and carried her into the bedroom for round two.

Price leaned back in the chair and studied Sable sleeping soundly in the hotel bed the morning after. She stirred, and he was by her side as she opened her eyes.

"Price?" She looked up, startled.

"Good morning, beautiful." He sat by her side. "About last night," he began softly. "We shifted gears, but our bond is non-negotiable. Understand? You're my air. You're my everything, Sable. Your happiness is the priority. So, if this arrangement ever gets too . . ."

She wiped away a tear, and he wiped away the rest. "Price, you'll always be the one. For life."

"Yes." He kissed her hand. "For life."

Chapter 11

"Priscilla Lee, is that you?" he asked.

After forty years, two months, and three days, the raspy voice alone made her freeze. *Lord Jesus, please don't let it be. Don't let it be.* Wilson Storm's face was the last face she wanted to see. He had pimped her out when she couldn't pay rent. Eventually, she left the state of Alabama, abandoned her family, even changed her name. Now, in one nauseating twist of fate, her past had caught up with her. No sacrifice was too great to keep it hidden. She turned around slowly, her heart bungee jumping to her toes.

"Sorry, ma'am." He tipped his hat at her, his left eye as lazy as ever. "I thought you were someone else."

Lilly hurried home, surrounded by whispering shadows and a lifetime of nightmares. She had always known that this day would come. She just wasn't ready. Wilson hadn't recognized her. Or had he? More importantly, what was he doing in New York? The Big Apple wasn't big enough for both of them. What price must she pay to secure her unraveling respectability? Padding her prayer account, Lilly spent an extra half hour on her knees before turning in. Still, sleep eluded her that night as she sought the fetal position. Even on that muggy summer night, her cold, sweaty body trembled. What would people think if they knew?

Her mind raced back to another lifetime. She was Priscilla Lee Patton back then, and she was late with the rent. At fifteen years old, she was a runaway. She reached inside her brassiere for the wad of bills and counted it again. She had exactly thirty-seven dollars to her name—one twenty, two fives, and seven damp and wilted singles. Then she removed her right shoe to reveal her other hiding place. Underneath the insole were five quarters, four dimes, and eight pennies, which gave her a grand total of I-can't-pay-my-damn-rent. Again.

What was she going to do this time? Wilson Storm, her landlord, had let her slide a few months ago when she allowed him a quick feel of her breasts, the old, fat fart. If she closed her eyes, he didn't look so bad, but he was as funky as the night was long. Each time she was short thereafter, his drive-bys got longer and longer. One month, when she was completely broke, Wilson took all that she had.

Their affair lasted three months, until he grew tired of her and kicked her out on her behind. He then suggested that she join a local whorehouse a few towns away. Priscilla Lee Patton took his advice and was never broke another day in her life.

Day one in the brothel was an education. Madam Magnolia had even given her a quiz. Priscilla Lee learned what to do, what not to do, what to say, and what not to say from the flaming redheaded maven. Nine girls welcomed her. Priscilla Lee steered clear of the tenth. There was no love lost between Priscilla Lee and Abby, and everyone knew it. Most of the brothel stories were the same. They had fallen on desperate times, couldn't find a job, so they resorted to the world's oldest money maker.

Priscilla Lee shared a room with Dakota, and they became fast friends. They'd stay up half the night painting their nails red and experimenting with different hairstyles. Dakota hipped her quick to her bag of tricks. For the first few days, Priscilla Lee was off limits to the men. She sat in the large living room solely as an observer, watching the men come in and make their selections before the girls led them away. Some men were regulars and had their favorites. Others enjoyed a variety or wanted a threesome. As long as the request wasn't too kinky, Madam Magnolia obliged them.

Filled with the names and sexual preferences of some of the town's most prominent men, Madam Magnolia's little black book was kept under lock and key. Even though Priscilla Lee was far from home, she soon began recognizing a few of the faces that frequented the brothel from TV and local newspapers. And what she didn't learn from the media, the girls filled her in. It amazed her how much they were willing to pay for a couple of hours' worth of diversion.

Priscilla Lee was initiated into the life by none other than Wilson Storm. Seeing him again was a slap in the face. She thought that when he kicked her to the curb, he was gone from her life. Evi-damn-dently not so. Unbeknownst to her, he was the final exam. Gritting her teeth, she led him to the back room. She wasn't about to ask him how he liked it, but she already knew. Priscilla Lee undressed him while fending off his attempts to kiss her lips. He finally grabbed the back of her neck, this close to securing mouth-to-mouth.

"You let me kiss you before," he told her.

She struggled to break free. "Things change."

"I was your first. Remember?"

"Don't remind me." For Priscilla Lee, the session couldn't end fast enough. She dug deep and allowed her mind to take her to another place. She lay on her back, gazing up at the ceiling as she did what she was paid to do.

Sleeping with Wilson Storm proved that Priscilla Lee could separate business from her personal feelings, and that was all Madam Magnolia needed to know. Wilson collected his usual finder's fee, and Priscilla Lee found a new home. She promised herself she wasn't there to stay. She was simply passing through.

Eight months in, Priscilla Lee was sick of pricks. She had had enough. One of the girls suggested she might be expecting. Priscilla Lee knew better than that. She had been way too careful to even smell pregnant. She couldn't take it anymore. Besides, she had managed to put away enough of a little nest egg that she didn't have to. It was time to step.

She slept lighter just knowing that she was spending her last night there. She had already told Madam Magnolia and the girls, and they wished her well. They even threw her a little farewell party, complete with ice cream and cake after the last john left that evening. Everyone attended except Abby.

Priscilla Lee woke up that morning feeling like a freed slave. Every nerve in her body tingled with anticipation. She had already bought a one-way ticket to New York, primed for a fresh start in the most exciting city in the world. She retrieved her one suitcase from the bedroom closet, careful not to disturb a sleeping Dakota as she closed the squeaky door. Smiling, she unlocked the suitcase and reached for the new handbag she had purchased a couple of weeks ago from the department store uptown. The matching wallet was there—but all her money was gone. Her smile evaporated.

"Dakota," she screamed. "Wake up." She ran over to Dakota's bed and shook her.

Startled, Dakota jumped from her sleep. "What's wrong?"

"All my money's gone. All of it." Priscilla Lee ran her fingers through her hair.

"You probably just misplaced it. You're always hiding things from yourself," Dakota reminded her.

"No, Dakota. It's gone. See for yourself."

"When's the last time you saw it?"

"Last night, before the party," Priscilla Lee told her.

"Are you thinking what I'm—?"

Before Dakota could get the words out of her mouth, Priscilla Lee had bolted from the room. Dakota was right behind her as she barged into Abby's bedroom.

"Bitch, gimme my money. You stole my money."

Abby looked at her like she was crazy. "Dakota, you better get your friend or—"

"Or what?" Priscilla Lee demanded.

"Oh, so you big and bad enough to come into my room and call me a thief?" She stood eye to eye with Priscilla.

"Yeah, I'm big and bad enough, bitch."

Abby laughed. "Bring it."

Priscilla Lee tore the lamp out of the socket and smashed Abby in the head before she knew what hit her. Abby went down momentarily but came up swinging. Dakota tried to separate them, but she was no match for two feuding females. It took Madam Magnolia and a few of the other girls to pull them apart.

"You'll regret this, you red barracuda-toed, lowlife bitch," Abby spewed.

"Ready for another lamp shade?"

"Keep talking," Abby told her.

"Enough," Madam Magnolia told them both. "Priscilla Lee, come with me. Abby, I want to see you downstairs in my office in ten minutes."

Priscilla Lee followed Madam Magnolia to her office. Moments later, the doorbell rang. Madam Magnolia rose from her desk, shaking her head as she walked the short distance to answer the door. It was Ian, one of Abby's regulars.

"Ian, this is really a bad time. Do you mind coming back later?"

"Sorry, Maggie, I'm here on official business. I understand that there was an altercation here earlier, and I'm here to arrest Miss Priscilla Lee Patton."

"Oh, shit," Priscilla Lee said. The officer handcuffed her wrists and read her Miranda rights as Abby watched from the top of the stairs.

"Asshole," Priscilla Lee said as Ian led her away.

"Jailbird," Abby shot back, laughing. "Enjoy that bread and water, girl. Your big behind could stand to drop a few pounds."

Madam Magnolia closed the door behind them as the other girls gathered around the living room window, watching until the police car faded from sight.

Priscilla Lee spent the night in jail. The charges were dropped in the morning when Madam Magnolia's hidden camera revealed that Abby was indeed a thief. Two things that Madam Magnolia didn't tolerate were lying and stealing. Abby had to go. Unfortunately, she managed to take half of Priscilla Lee's money with her. Priscilla Lee was back to square one—a whorehouse heifer just passing through.

Chapter 12

Tootsie arrived home after a long freakin' day at work. She turned off the radio and sat behind the wheel for a few moments, collecting her thoughts. Another patient had filed a complaint against her, and the boss issued a formal warning. He didn't give a damn about her partial hearing loss. He refused to tolerate unnecessary aggression at the Dental Den.

She stepped inside the house in time to catch the tail end of her mother's phone conversation.

"I don't care what you do, Wilson. All the churches in Queens, and you end up in mine. I better not see you in One Way no more. Stay away from my church, and don't call this house ever again. You got that?" Lilly slammed the phone down.

"Who was that, Mama?"

"Oh, you scared me." Looking like she'd seen a ghost, she grabbed her heart. "I didn't hear you come in. Damn telemarketers. Wait a minute. I thought we were on that do-not-call list."

"We are," Tootsie insisted.

"Well, then, somebody needs reminding. I have a good mind to sit down and write the mayor a letter. This don't make no kinda sense."

"All right, Mama." Tootsie said over her shoulder. "I'll drop it in the mail in the morning." She squelched a yawn.

"No, daughter, I'm sending this letter signature required, and I'm emailing him too. That's the only way to go, you know."

"Okay, Mama. Whatever you say." Tootsie had too much on her mind to worry about a damn telemarketer. She hadn't heard from Adonis in over a week, longer if she didn't count that quickie just-touching-base text he had sent her. What was she to do?

Tootsie settled herself inside her tiny bedroom, savoring the peace only a locked door could bring under Lilly's roof. She eased her body onto the bed, the mattress nearly folding in two. Was it so wrong to want to see Adonis? Just because she didn't believe in cherry popping before marriage didn't mean she couldn't use a little male companionship. After thirty-five years, come on, Lord. Hell, her hairline was racing to the finish line behind her ears, and the doctor had doubled her blood pressure medicine last month. Now her meal ticket was in jeopardy. The Dental Den was her third employer that year. She already had two complaints against her, and she was still on probation.

Tootsie picked up the phone to call Adonis. Her mother would kill her if she suspected wickedness in Tootsie's thoughts. She ended the call. Who made up the damn dating rules anyway? She wouldn't let them stop her. Again, Tootsie picked up the phone to call Adonis before she lost her nerve.

It started ringing. Too late to turn back now. Even if she hung up, her number would still register on his caller ID. Why hadn't she blocked her number? But maybe then he wouldn't bother picking up. Five rings . . . then six. At least he hadn't sent her straight to voicemail. Good sign.

"Hello?" he answered.

"Hey, Adonis, it's Tootsie."

"What's good?" he asked her.

Tootsie thought fast. "I got two tickets to see the Comedy Crew. Wanna come?"

"At the Garden?" he asked.

"Yeah, Friday night."

"Love to. I missed them last time they came to New York."

Tootsie could almost see that tight body through the phone. "Great. Well, I'll talk to you later . . ." Her voice trailed off.

"Wait a minute. Hold up, Tootsie. I've been meaning to call you, but my schedule's been tight."

"I understand," she told him.

"I feel like a teenager. I miss you, and I need to see you. I can't stop thinking about you, and we just met. Crazy, right?"

She laughed. "I feel the same way."

"What are you doing tonight?"

"Oh, I already made plans." *Hmmph,* she wasn't that desperate.

"How about tomorrow night?" Adonis asked her.

"Sorry."

"Guess I'll just have to wait till Friday. Maybe we can do dinner after the show."

"Okay." She was so ready to be wined and dined.

"Pick you up around eight?"

"Yes." She blushed as she hung up. Oh, my goodness. He wanted her, too. In the twinkling of an eye, her luck had changed. Could her marital status be far behind? A smile graced her lips as Tootsie re-lived the day their paths first crossed on the Ave. If it hadn't been for Burger King's buy-one, get-one-free Whopper promotion, she never would have been in the area. Look at God.

Sighing, Tootsie got to work. Making those Comedy Crew tickets appear would be true magic. She reached for her pressure pills, popping two. Just as she suspected, the cheap seats were all gone. Only the pricey ones remained. Tootsie couldn't see herself spending five hundred dollars on two concert tickets, but if they got her and Adonis one step closer to the altar, the concert would be well worth the investment. She reached for her wallet, grabbed her credit card, and completed the transaction before she lost her nerve.

Tootsie desperately needed new lingerie and a new outfit for her date with Adonis. Just because he wouldn't be getting any didn't mean she couldn't feel hot. She made plans to meet Bubbles at Macy's for their one-day sale, but she was held up by construction on the Conduit, making her nearly an hour late. On top of that, she was down to one bar on her phone and couldn't get in touch with Bubbles.

When they finally met up, Bubbles was on the phone with her husband. "I told you. I'm in the mall waiting for Tootsie . . . Yes, Hayden, I'm in Sunrise Mall . . . No, she's not here yet . . . I don't know. She's probably tied up in traffic. Now, if I were—"

Tootsie tapped her on the shoulder. Bubbles jumped slightly, spinning around in surprise.

"There you are. Here, say hello to my husband." She passed the phone to Tootsie before she could say no.

"Hi, Deacon, how are you? Uh-huh . . . okay. After that? Ashley Stewart . . . You too. Buh-bye. Here's Bubbles." Tootsie passed the phone back.

"All right, and dinner's in the fridge. Just heat it up in the microwave . . . okay, yeah . . . all right . . . uh-huh. Look, I know my way home," she insisted, hanging up.

Tootsie was amused. "Oh my gosh, does he smell your—?"

"Pain in the ass." Bubbles cut her off and shook her head.

"Well, at least you get it on the regular," Tootsie pointed out.

"Honey, puhleez. Ain't that much beef in the world."

On the day of the show, Tootsie did what she had to do. She sped through her last few clients, muting their moans and groans. Tootsie knew she'd hear complaints from her boss Monday morning, but what's a marriage-minded, thirty-five-year-old virgin to do?

When she got home, her mother was on the phone. She was so busy arguing, Lilly didn't hear her come in. She'd been on the phone a lot lately, but Tootsie didn't have time for her mother's drama. Besides, Lilly would be okay after two boxes of cookies and a pint of Rocky Road.

Tootsie didn't have time for her mother's drama. She had more important things on her agenda, like getting as beautiful as possible for the night Adonis would realize he couldn't live without her. She'd had her hair done during her lunch hour, and her nails were polished to perfection. She even suffered through her first Brazilian. It was Bubbles' idea. Talk about torture.com. She wished her dental patients would file another complaint. Punk-ass suckers.

Although a nice, long shower relaxed her, Tootsie was sweating before the bedroom door closed behind her. She sat on the bed and reached for the box of tissues on her nightstand, nearly knocking it over. If she didn't pull herself together, she'd be a nervous wreck. Slowly, she counted to twenty and steadied her breathing before blotting the beads of sweat from her face and neck.

Tootsie checked her phone for messages from Adonis. Not a one. Damn, the negro could have at least called her by now. This night came with a five-hundred-dollar price tag, not including the lingerie and new perfume she had splurged on.

She walked across the room and opened the window, hoping the fresh air would ease some of the tension that had crept inside her head. It was a mild evening—good for snuggling if you had it like that.

A text came through from Adonis.

Can't wait till eight!

Tootsie pinched herself. They were still on. She checked her watch. It was a little past six. Standing in the mirror, she slipped into her new red cheetah print lingerie, thankful that the chocolate mudslide brownies she had eaten earlier in the week hadn't added more dimples to her bodacious thighs. She turned around in the mirror to gaze at her rear view.

By 6:55, Tootsie was dressed in a black jumpsuit with a red camisole peeking through. Sweat was the only problem that kept her from getting dressed earlier, and just in those five minutes alone, she could feel the camisole begin to stick to her back. Where was Adonis?

She waited for what felt like forever, trying to call several times. At this rate, they were going to be seriously late for the show. She reached for another tissue to wipe her brow as she checked her watch. It was eight fifteen. She groaned. Friday night traffic was always a mother. Still, she comforted herself with the thought that most concerts didn't start on time anyway. They'd be okay.

By eight thirty, perspiration dripping from her wet armpits and back forced Tootsie to remove her jumpsuit. The camisole came off next. She kicked off her black patent leather sandals before stretching out across her beloved bed. It felt so good underneath her, an old friend that never let her down. Sure, the mattress sagged, but her bed always had her back. Together, they were the perfect cocktail, and she quickly succumbed, drifting off to sleep.

Somewhere around eleven thirty, the phone rang, catapulting her out of a deep sleep. Jumping up, she answered it.

"Hey, Tootsie. What's going on?" It was Adonis.

The second she heard his voice, she hung up. That man had just caused her to blow five hundred dollars. Adonis called her back. Once again, she hung up on him. The third time, Tootsie sent Adonis's behind straight to voicemail. She punched her pillow and went back to sleep. He got the message.

Bright and early Monday morning, she got the message, too. Her boss called her into his office. He put her at ease with questions about her family, weekend, etc. Relaxing under the ice breaker, she even joked about planning a vacation. Tootsie was completely blindsided by his lunge for the jugular. He informed her he was suspending her without pay for thirty days. Her file overflowed with patient complaints. He turned a deaf ear to her claims of partial hearing loss. If he received so much as a hint of another client complaint against her, she was fired. She signed the required forms, and their meeting ended just as abruptly as it began. She got up from the chair, brushed herself off, and walked out of his office. Amidst snickering coworkers, she grabbed her belongings and bounced.

Tootsie's savings wouldn't last forever. No paycheck for four weeks was devastating enough, without adding her mother's lip to the equation. Three days lapsed before Tootsie admitted to Lilly that she'd been suspended.

Later that afternoon, Lilly stuck her head in the doorway of Tootsie's room. "Come on. Let's go to Popeye's—my treat. It'll make you feel better."

Tootsie exhaled. One less thing to worry about.

The aroma of fried chicken and biscuits hit hard and fast as they entered the fast-food eatery on Springfield and North Conduit. Lilly grabbed a table while Tootsie placed the orders.

Their timing was perfect. Everything was fresh from the oven and piping hot as they sank their teeth into Popeye's finest. Smiling, Tootsie shoveled a forkful of red beans and rice into her mouth. Maybe the month off would do her some good after all. She could flip the script and call it a vacation. Work always did interfere with her life.

Lilly was busy with a wing, sucking like a human vacuum cleaner. Several people turned around to stare, including an old, lazy-eyed man who got up out of his seat and approached them. Tootsie nearly lost her appetite. Almost.

"I'd know that sucking anywhere. Priscilla Lee, it's been a long time. How are you?"

"It's Lilly now," she told him sharply.

"That's what I meant. You know the memory is the third thing to go. How are you?" he repeated.

"Fine." She refused to meet his gaze.

"And who is this beauty?" He turned to get a better look at Tootsie.

"My daughter."

"Aren't you going to introduce us?"

"Tootsie, this is Wilson Storm."

"Pleasure to meet you." He grinned, his yellow teeth matching the Crayola box of her youth.

Tootsie quickly looked away. She could have a field day in his mouth. It wasn't pretty.

"Enjoy the rest of your meal," he told them before returning to his table.

"Mama, who was that man?" Tootsie frowned, watching him walk away.

"Just one of Mama's seasons," she said simply.

Chapter 13

After a turbulent flight, Price and Sable's plane touched down in sunny Kingston, Jamaica, and their vacation began. They grabbed their carry-ons, exited the plane, and boarded the rear seats of an awaiting shuttle, greeting other vacationers in the process. After being dropped off at the all-inclusive Hush St. Regis couple's resort, they checked into their suite.

"Hungry?" Price asked Sable.

"I am."

"Let's check out that bar and grill," he suggested.

"Okay."

"And wear something grown and sexy," he added.

"You're the boss." She grinned.

Price joined her in the shower, sliding his fingers up and down her soap-slippery body until he grew hard in her hands. He squeezed a generous amount of conditioning shampoo in his palm and began massaging it into her crown, creating a thick, frothy lather that soon trailed down her neck and back. Under the rain shower, he rinsed her hair until all traces of shampoo had disappeared. He backed her against the shower's rear wall and teased her until she begged him to make love to her, but he showed no mercy. Instead, he grabbed a plush white towel from a nearby rack to cover himself and walked out. Not another word was spoken.

Sable reached for Price's favorite perfume and scented lotion, enveloping her body in a layer of her husband's liking. She sat at the vanity table and slipped into strappy black sandals before applying makeup.

Fully dressed and with a drink in tow, Price watched as she secured her hair in an updo and donned a pair of shoulder-duster earrings. Catching his reflection in the mirror, she refused to meet his gaze.

"Beautiful." He bent down, kissing her neck from behind. "And all mine."

Their eyes met in the glass.

Finally, she turned to face him. "Am I?"

"Hmmph, you better be," he warned her.

Sable stood and slipped into her husband's favorite little black dress without saying another word.

He zipped her up from behind and extended his hand. "Let's go."

They snacked and sipped complimentary rum punch at the bar while their meal was being prepared. Sable was hungry, but not for food. Price gestured, and they moved to a table that opened nearby. The server came, and they noshed on an assortment of appetizers.

Price looked up and grinned. Sable followed his gaze, unable to believe her eyes.

"Hey, y'all." Chantel beamed as she and David walked toward them.

Price stood and gave David a fist bump. "Man, I was about to bust. You don't know how hard it was keeping this surprise a secret."

David laughed as Chantel and Sable exchanged a warm hug, and the four squeezed into the booth. The server returned with rum punch for David and Chantel before taking their orders.

"So, what's good?" David asked Price.

Price glanced at Chantel to his left and grinned. "Oh, it's all good."

"Yeah, mon," the server agreed, grinning as he left.

"So how was your flight?" Sable asked Chantel as she popped another spicy jerk salmon bite into her mouth.

"Smooth as silk." Chantel smiled.

The server returned with their meals, and David and Chantel got busy. "Something about island air that just makes everything taste better," David admitted.

Price nodded in agreement. "It's time." They raised their glass in a toast. "Let the fun begin."

David stood, extending his palm to Sable. After one last confirmation glance at her husband, she placed her hand in David's before walking out of the lounge. Hand in hand, they explored the resort, making note of every single couple-friendly nook and cranny. They ended up in a tiny, semi-dark room in a deserted area of the resort. He closed the door.

"Ooh, where have you taken me, Pastor Dante?"

"Let's just say we're not in Kansas anymore. Say my name."

"David."

"Again."

"David," she said softly.

"I love the way you say my name," he whispered before stroking her chin with his thumb. He wrapped his hand around her neck and pulled her in, his lips inches from hers.

Their breathing became one. He took another step toward her, and she edged back, which landed her seat on top of a desk, facing him, her legs slightly spread. Wrapping his arms around her waist, David closed the gap between them by sliding her to the desk's edge. Sable grabbed his shoulders to steady herself, electricity surging through her system.

He unzipped her dress before pulling it up and over her head. He tasted her first with his eyes as she watched her husband's favorite dress fall to the floor.

She couldn't take her eyes off his. Slowly, he leaned in and planted a kiss on her mouth. Their lips spiraled them into places they had only dreamed of. In the semi-darkness, he unhooked her bra, covering her with more desire. Next, he peeled off her panties so effortlessly she barely had time to take her next breath.

David removed his jacket and unbuttoned his shirt, using them to cover the table. Perched on David's shirt, Sable sat completely naked, save for her strappy stilettos. David released Sable's bobby pins, setting her hair free. Her eyes were glued to every ripple in his flesh, his eyes to her. Slowly, he took it in—lingering over every ripe inch—before easing them both down onto the desktop.

His hungry mouth sought hers while cradling the nape of her neck with his taut bicep. She spread her legs as his hand trailed down her body. He parted her precious jewel with his thumbs, pampering and enticing her hidden treasure with his fingers until desire drizzled like syrup down her thighs.

He stood for a moment. "Look at me, Sable."

She met his gaze.

"I want to lick it."

His words alone nearly made her cum, but somehow, she found the strength to slide her calves over his shoulders. Kneeling, David plunged his tongue into her womanhood. "I could eat you all night."

He took his time, and her body glistened.

Finally, David stood. He unzipped his fly and entered her, releasing their unconsummated desire, enslaving their unbridled lust. Sable closed her eyes and gave in, savoring this excruciating pleasure as she surrendered to every inch of his massiveness.

"Do you want me to stop?"

"No," she moaned. "Don't stop. Please . . . don't stop."

Approaching footsteps from the hall only heightened their passion as the desk squeaked sweetly underneath them. Pastor Dante covered her mouth with his hand, shushing softly in her ear as she came. The footsteps passed, and Pastor Dante came, too.

After several rum punch refills, Price and Chantel called it a night and headed upstairs to his suite. Within moments, they were naked on the bed, and Chantel enjoyed a much-needed massage. Price stood and summoned Chantel into the shower for an intense, deep tissue. Wet, naked, and dripping with desire, they headed back to the bedroom, where their mutual pleasuring continued. Drenched in sweat, they collapsed back onto the sheets and dozed off as the faint sounds of David and Sable's lovemaking from the adjoining suite reached a feverish pitch.

The next morning after a hearty breakfast, they doubled up on sunscreen, changed into swimsuits, and headed to the pool. After a quick dip, the women spent the rest of the afternoon reading trashy romance novels and urban fiction. They worked on their cinnamon toast tans, while their husbands took full advantage of the pool's hypnotic blue waters and swim-up bar.

Chapter 14

Bubbles' phone had been pinging like crazy ever since she tracked Price leaving Juice's that night, so she knew he was up to something. The problem was that she had yet to locate those turquoise teal crystal stiletto peep-toe pumps. So, after church, her search resumed. It ought to be against the law for Google to have so many results for one shoe search. That's why her girl Tootsie was helping to narrow the field. Bubbles didn't care how long she had to look. She had been determined to get those shoes ever since she overheard Sable mention that they were her favorites.

Somewhere around midnight, God smiled on Bubbles. They were at Saks Fifth Avenue. Just her luck. Leave it to Sable to step foot in the one shoe department in the city that boasted its own pricey zip code. The few dollars she had stashed away in her mad money account couldn't cover one heel, let alone two shoes, but she had to have them. Dare she borrow another cent against her KMA account? They had only four pairs left in her size. They'd fit like a glove everywhere but in her budget. Hayden would kick her teeth in if he knew she'd spent that kind of money on shoes.

Right before her eyes, the number of shoes dropped to three. Bubbles' heart was racing, her head pounding. She logged off her computer, stretched, and called it a night. Sliding under the covers beside her husband, she enjoyed only a few moments of peace before Hayden grabbed her by the neck in a chokehold. Would the madness ever end? Bubbles freed herself, slipping all the way to the other side of their full-sized bed. No place to run.

Control was his middle name. She should have known his rat bastard ass was controlling early on, the way he hung on to her every word, depositing them into his memory bank. At first, she was flattered by this attentiveness, until he began using her own words against her. Before long, he began tracking her every move. She soon learned to guard her words.

Within thirty seconds, Hayden had pinned her down to the mattress with one hand, while stripping off her robe with the other. With just a pair of pajamas between them, Bubbles was in for another night of pavement-pounding sex. She flinched as Hayden yanked off the cotton bottoms. Bubbles turned her gaze toward the nightstand. Hayden's passions were in perfect sync with the glowing second hand of the clock. She closed her eyes. Soon, her turquoisey-teal crystal stiletto struts were in perfect sync with his thrusts, too. She smiled in the dark. Those turquoisey-teal crystal stiletto peep-toe pumps would be hers come daybreak. She'd make the leap. After all the crap his trifling behind put her through, she so deserved them.

The minute Hayden drove off the next morning, Bubbles' feet hit the floor. She stared at her computer in disbelief. Somewhere between midnight and when Hayden left to go to work, the last three pairs of shoes had been sold. She felt sick to her stomach. That damn Sable had won again. How come she always got the green light? If it weren't for bad luck . . .

"You should have snatched them up the second you found them," Tootsie told her over lunch in Manhattan. "Time is a bomb. What's wrong with you?"

"I know. I was this close." Bubbles used her fingers for emphasis.

Tootsie shook her head as she bit into her burger. "I don't understand you."

"Sometimes I don't understand myself," she admitted. That Barbie doll pony-tailed Sable had beaten her again.

"Hey, let's stop by Saks while we're here."

"My broke behind has no business stepping one toe in that store, let alone ten." Bubbles stirred her soda with the straw.

"Come on," Tootsie insisted. "What do you have to lose?"

Bubbles could not believe her luck. An hour later, she was staring down the throat of the turquoisey-teal crystal stiletto peep-toe pumps. She rubbed its shaft. The leather was soft as *buttah*. Bubbles dared not look away. Funny, she thought as she viewed the shoes from various angles. They didn't look this high on Sable's feet. They had to be a good six inches, if not more. She wondered if she could even walk in them. She'd have to practice at home first. No use wobbling around the sanctuary like a crippled cat. She needed Sable to see her strutting her stuff down the church's catwalk like a supermodel in heat. Could she really pull off the fashionista look?

A serpent-like Tootsie snuck up from behind, whispering in her ear. "Don't let 'em slip away again. See if they have your size."

Bubbles tried to protest. "You want me casket sharp?"

"Come on, Bubbles. Life isn't long." Tootsie flagged down a sales associate. "Size eight, right?"

Bubbles nodded, digging her own grave. Part of her was relieved when the associate returned, shaking her head. "No eight, but I have an eight and a half."

"Damn," Bubbles said under her breath.

"She'll try it," Tootsie butted in, relieving the associate of the shoe box.

Bubbles sat as Tootsie passed her the shoebox. Cursing under her breath, she removed the lid and opened the tissue paper, exposing her fantasy. She gasped at the possibilities, feeling slightly lightheaded.

"Try them on," Tootsie told her.

Bubbles held her breath. She removed the wad of tissue and cardboard from each shoe before slipping them on her feet. She stood. They were a tad too big, sliding off her feet as she walked. They were definitely wearing her.

"Too big. Why did I even bother?"

"That's nothing," Tootsie insisted. "All you have to do is buy a pair of those insoles from the drugstore—you know the gel ones they advertise on TV all the time—and they'll fit like a glove."

"At this price, they should already fit like a glove." Bubbles switched positions as she took another look at herself in the mirror.

"Your call." Tootsie squeezed into a nearby chair. "A fool and her shoes are soon parted. When is your time to shine? How long are you going to let Sable trump you?"

That did it. Bubbles caved. Those shoes would put her on the church radar. She spun around in the mirror one last time, her purse slung over her shoulder. They had seduced her into a ride home. She'd wear them this Sunday. She signaled the sales associate and met her at the register, praying that the available balance on her credit card was enough to cover the shoes. It wasn't. Her eyes were bigger than her knock-off wallet. She breathed a sigh of relief when the third credit card's balance was enough.

Bubbles shook her head as she explained to the sales associate that her assistant had forgotten to make a trip to the bank.

"Hmmm." The sales associate didn't crack a smile.

"It's so hard to find good help these days," Bubbles continued, her voice dropping an octave.

"You get what you pay for," she said, handing Bubbles her package.

Bubbles raised her nose on the way out. If Sable didn't comment on how good Bubbles looked Sunday morning, it would be because Sable was dying with envy inside.

Like a little girl on Christmas Eve, Bubbles squirmed with anticipation. She lay in bed Saturday night, awaiting the next morning's enviable looks headed her way. Having already chosen the perfect outfit— off-white suit and icy pale turquoise silk blouse—to showcase her turquoisey-teal crystal stiletto peep-toe stunners, she counted down the hours.

She rolled onto her side and looked at the form in the darkness. He was fast asleep. Bubbles sank into her pillow. She wouldn't have to worry about him tonight. The Lord was on her side. She mouthed a thank-you.

Early Sunday morning, Bubbles stepped out of the shower, blowing herself a kiss. Like a model prepping for a fashion show, she wanted to strut. It wouldn't take a village to make her catwalk fierce.

Even Hayden commented on how good she looked. "New shoes?" he asked on the way out.

"Uh-uh," she lied, glancing out the window. Saturday night, after Hayden went to sleep, she had carefully attached red masking tape to the soles and heel lifts of the shoes for an effortless return. It was an old wardrobing trick the women in her family knew well.

After what seemed like an eternity, Bubbles and Hayden pulled up into the church parking lot. He turned off the engine. They both got out of the car and walked up the steps.

Bubbles had her entrance all planned. "You go ahead," she told her husband. "I need to go to the ladies' room and fix my slip."

"Don't be too long," he said, winking.

Once inside, Bubbles headed down the stairs leading to the ladies' lounge. She wanted to give her outfit one last look-over. The lounge was empty. Pleased with her reflection in the full-length mirror, Bubbles smiled. She had it going on. She was ready to walk the walk and be on the tip of everyone's lips. Though her toe cleavage wasn't quite like Sable's, her supermodel attitude would shoot her through the roof. As she climbed the stairs to the first floor, a couple of women coming down the steps noticed her feet and gasped.

"Oh, my goodness, gorgeous shoes," one exclaimed.

"I love 'em," the other agreed.

"Thank you," she replied as she continued up the stairs. It was a good day to be Bubbles Legree. As she neared the top, she glanced back to see the women still admiring her shoes. "Enjoy the service," she told them piously.

Bubbles hung out in the church's foyer, killing time. Was Sable here yet? From where she stood, she couldn't see if Sable was seated, but she was rarely late. Bubbles glanced across the aisle at Hayden. He turned in his seat, looking for her as the choir marched in, singing. She checked her watch. She had already left Hayden alone longer than she knew he was comfortable with. She would definitely hear his mouth.

It was time to walk the walk. Runway ready, Bubbles waited for the choir to be seated and for the hallelujahs to subside before she made her grand entrance. She was cooked and ready to be served. She took a deep breath and proceeded down the middle aisle. No doubt about it, Bubbles Legree had finally arrived. She slowed her stroll, savoring the delicious stares. It was a sin to look this good.

Bubbles reached her husband's side, her lips pursed. Where the hell was Sable? Bubbles snatched up the paper fan from the back of the pew in front of her. Where the hell was she? Sable rarely missed service. It was just her luck that Sable would pick that Sunday of all days to skip church.

Hayden wrapped his arm around Bubbles' shoulders as he whispered in her ear. "Where were you?"

"Wardrobe malfunction. Nothing to worry about," she reassured him. "Everything's under control."

"Good," he told her as they stood for the prayer of confession.

Bubbles had only one request for the Lord—that Sable would get her behind in church before service ended. She didn't even care that one of the assistant pastors was bringing the word that morning, even though that in itself was quite rare. Her eyes fixated on her watch more than the pulpit. The service was halfway over, and still no Sable. Out of her peripheral vision, Bubbles noticed someone in Sable's seat. Maybe she was sitting upstairs in the overflow room.

The rest of the service passed in a fog. She and Hayden rose to their feet for the benediction, and then the congregation was dismissed. Slowly, the couple made their way to the rear. Hayden stopped a few times to talk to several of the brethren as he and Bubbles made their way down the church steps.

With her hand in Hayden's, Bubbles panned the crowd for Sable. Hayden finished speaking and took another step down just as Bubbles turned her head back and upward one last time in search of Sable. In that instant, Bubbles lost her balance, twisted her ankle, and slid down the remaining four steps. As she hit the cement, all she could think about was the shoes. Her bruised behind was a mere afterthought.

Hayden helped her up. They continued toward the parking lot with Bubbles hobbling all the way to the car. She couldn't afford to put any extra weight on that right heel. They were damaged enough. Yet, as she removed the tape from the shoe's underside later that afternoon, she realized that the soles were the least of her problems.

The next morning, she packed up the shoes and headed to the shoe repair. The owner, a short, white, elderly man with thick horn-rimmed glasses, assured her he'd have her shoes looking like new, but that he had a couple of jobs ahead of hers. She breathed a sigh of relief, though leaving the shoes overnight was out of the question. Bubbles sat and waited. And waited.

Bubbles watched customers come and go—some dropping off shoes or handbags, others picking them up. As the steady flow of traffic kept revolving, she checked her watch several times, popping a mint in her mouth to quiet her growling stomach.

Finally, the job was done. The owner motioned for Bubbles to come to the register. She examined the shoes. They did look like new. Even the slight scratch near the toe had been smoothed into oblivion. Humming, Bubbles paid the owner, leaving a hefty tip.

Two hours later, Bubbles was back in Manhattan and next in line at Saks. The wide-eyed, curly-haired brunette looked gullible enough. Bubbles couldn't help but smile. She'd be on her way in no time. Just as she approached the register, another woman came to replace the wide-eyed curly-haired brunette, advising her that it was her lunchtime. Shit. Bubbles stood face-to-face with the same sales associate who had rung up the original sale.

She inspected the turquoisey-teal crystal stiletto peep-toe pumps.

"I'm sorry, but we cannot accept your return."

"What do you mean, you can't accept my return?" Bubbles stared her down. "It's only been a week."

"Ma'am, clearly these shoes have been worn. Look at them. And look at these cheap lifts. Our designers never skimp on quality."

Bubbles held up her hand, dismissing her. "Let me see the manager."

"Lucky you. I am the manager," she replied.

Bubbles checked her name tag. She looked like a Becki. She stared her down.

"Look." Becki used her hand for emphasis. "Our return policy clearly states that returned merchandise must be in its original condition and cannot be worn, damaged, or soiled. Look at these shoes. They've been worn, and here at Saks, we do not take wardrobing lightly."

Bubbles overheard two women behind her whispering.

"Sure, they all want to look the part, but can they afford it?"

"Stay in your lane," the other added.

Bubbles re-bagged her shoes. "This isn't over. I'll write the CEO of Saks if I have to."

"His address is on our website. Have a good day." Becki motioned for the next customer.

When Bubbles returned home that evening, Hayden was waiting. She barely had time to close the door behind her before the questions began. His expression said it all.

"How was your day?" he began as he approached her. He was a piranha circling his prey.

"It was good." She reached for her nape to ease the sudden pain that shot down her back.

"Just good? Not wonderful or fabulous?"

"It was fine."

"And how was it last week?"

"I . . . I don't recall."

"Don't we sound guilty? According to the credit card company, you were living the fabulous life—shoe shopping at Saks, lunching on Fifth Avenue. Is that about right?"

She turned her back on him to collect her thoughts. Everything she said from that point on would just further infuriate him. She knew it, and he knew it. She let him do all the talking.

"Look at me. Who do you think you are, one of the Atlanta Housewives? You ain't Gone with the Wind fabulous." He threw some old shade.

Bubbles wished she could mute his ass. She turned around just in time for her cheek to meet his fist. She prayed the marks would fade by Sunday. Visible bruises would threaten his precious rep, and then he'd really jack her up.

"That's for leaving the house without your damn brain." He grabbed her by the throat, nearly choking the life out of her. Bubbles watched a faint shadow of a grin eclipse his face as her eyes rolled back into her head. Like the cartoon coyote, she was down for the count. The last thing she thought of before blacking out was Sable Galore and those damn turquoise-teal crystal stiletto peep-toe pumps.

Hayden slamming the front door as he went off to work the next morning woke Bubbles up. Startled, she looked around for her phone. Though she was still sore from Hayden's beatdown, she got up gingerly and walked over to the dresser to retrieve it.

In her obsession to track down the pumps, she had accidentally deactivated Price's accounts and group chats. Now, they were hitting her phone and pinging with vengeance as she turned her phone back on.

What the . . .?

She showered and got to the airport. Her phone pinged again as the two couples touched down from their sneaky link vacation. Parked in arrivals, she waited, binoculars ready. They exited, relaxed as a summer breeze and looking like cinnamon toast. Sable and Chantel huddled together, laughing as if sharing a private joke.

Bubbles thought back to her grandmother's advice. When two women walk hand in hand, one is sleeping with the other one's man. From their body language, Bubbles sensed that they had swapped. When the heck did this happen? Shit. She'd been so busy obsessing over Sable and those doggone shoes when she should have kept a closer eye on Chantel. She was done calling her First Lady when it was evident that no honor was due. They all hugged goodbye and hopped into awaiting taxis, disappearing into traffic.

Seething, Bubbles clenched her teeth and drove off. *Hmmph, we'll see who gets the last laugh.*

She arrived home and got busy, setting up fake private social media accounts as "Chantel." She sent deep fake photos of Chantel and Price on the beach to Price's private page, anticipating his response.

He quickly DM'd the fake account with four words: REMOVE IMMEDIATELY OR ELSE.

She responded with three: OR ELSE WHAT?

He responded with two: CRAZY BITCH. Then he blocked her account.

Bubbles watched as he called Chantel. Bubbles quickly hacked into his phone log and disconnected the call. He called Chantel back, and Bubbles disconnected them again. By the time he sent Chantel a text, she had already gone into Chantel's phone and blocked him. Through the camera, she watched his expression darken as sweat formed on his nose and the vein in his neck protruded. While trying to contain her laughter, she allowed his third phone call attempt to go through.

"Chantel, are you stupid, or are you just dumb? And what the hell were you thinking?" he asked.

"What are you talking about?"

"The naked photos of us. That was a BS move."

"What photos? I don't even know what you're talking about."

"Oh, like you didn't just DM my private social media account?"

"No, I did not," she insisted. "Wait a minute. Send me a screenshot. Holy shit. That's not even me. I mean, it's my face, but I have a birthmark on my—Hold up."

"What's happening?"

"Gimme a sec. I just got an alert." She screenshotted the message and sent it to him. "I think someone hacked my account."

"Who?"

"How the hell would I know?" she snapped.

"But if these photos get leaked, we're all cooked. I hope nobody was spying on us at the resort."

"I'll delete the photos. Make sure you change all your passwords."

"I'll change mine too."

"And stay off social media for a while until we get to the bottom of this. You guys still have a landline?"

"Yeah, that may have been hacked too."

"You're right. Tell David we may have to cool things for a while."

"Crazy."

"Listen, I gotta run. Talk to you later."

They disconnected.

Bubbles couldn't help but laugh. Her new mission was to break up their cozy little covenant by any means necessary. She'd make Chantel look so crazy, so combative, so clumsy, so bad that he'd kick her to the curb and come running back to her. They didn't know who they were messing with, but they were about to FAFO.

Chapter 15

"You want me to marry who?" Tootsie asked her mother. "Wilson Storm? That old man we met in Popeye's that day? He's as old as spit. Mama, you done lost your mind."

Lilly took a deep breath. "Just listen to what I'm saying. You're a thirty-five-year-old virgin. In my day, you'd be an old maid. Let's face it. Men aren't exactly beating down the door to ask you out, let alone marry you. How many good years do you think you have left? I mean, really. Your loss is someone else's gain."

"You call that a gain? I don't see you jumping to it."

"Daughter, you need to calm down and think this through. As his wife, you'll be able to live well, and I guarantee you, you'll never have to work another day in your life."

"It's sex trafficking, Mama."

"You can make this work, Tootsie. Just think about it. You always say work interferes with your life. Does eating interfere with your life? Look at you. At the rate you're going, you won't even have a job."

Tootsie pushed herself away from the kitchen table. "I'm out."

Wilson Storm had called Lilly every night that week. If she couldn't convince her daughter to marry him, Lilly's time would be up. Wilson was threatening to expose her.

Lord, don't let him act on it.

Lilly leaned over in her green-and-white floral tent dress and pulled out the old cast-iron skillet from underneath the kitchen sink. She poured grease into the skillet and turned on the burner. Next, she washed, cut up, and seasoned the chicken, frying it to perfection in the hot oil. That, along with the leftover fried corn and okra and buttermilk biscuits, would set her right. She put her face in a bowl of ice cream and called it a night. The dishes could wait till the morning.

With her belly full, Lilly settled on the couch and flipped on the TV. Smiling, she slipped into a sugar coma. Occasionally, the sound of her own snoring broke her sleep. The ringing of the phone catapulted her awake. She sat up with a jolt.

Only after the call went to voicemail did she scramble to pick up the phone. It was Wilson Storm. Again. Tootsie didn't need to hear this. Lilly jumped up and grabbed the phone, cutting his recording short.

"What is it now?" she asked, her voice dripping with disgust.

"You're long on attitude, and I'm short on patience."

"It's after midnight. You know I need my beauty sleep."

"You're going to need more than that when I'm through with you."

"Your word against mine."

He laughed. "Priscilla Lee, I have more than words to back up my story. What do you have to back up yours?"

"You would have destroyed me by now if you could. You're wasting both our time. Goodbye." She slammed the phone in the cradle, but he called her right back.

"Haven't you ever wondered what happened to Madam Magnolia's little black book?"

Dead silence.

"That's more like it, Priscilla Lee. You know what I like to hear? Cooperation. I'll meet you at Big Smoke's BBQ Pit, say one o'clock. Sweet dreams."

Lilly hung up, shivering as she returned to the couch and reached for a blanket. The next thing she knew, she blinked, and it was morning.

Lilly took a quick bath and stepped out of the tub. No matter how often she bathed, she left a bathtub ring. Just another reminder that we are all made from the dust of the Earth.

More than ever, she needed a hearty breakfast. She whipped up a batch of buttermilk pancakes and hotlinks, eating in a race against the clock as she heard Tootsie's footsteps approaching. Where food was concerned, the Tasmanian devil had nothing on her.

Frantic to hide her morning indulgence, she nearly gagged on the last bit of sausage as it slid down her throat. She gulped down coffee to help it along before jumping up and stacking the dishes in the dishwasher. Tootsie appeared just as Lilly closed the door to the dishwasher. *Whew, that was close. Nap time.* One o'clock would arrive soon enough.

"You look like hell, Priscilla Lee," Wilson told her as they lunched at the popular Merrick eatery.

"Hmmmph, and you don't?" she mocked, shaking her head.

"Let's cut to the chase. You know what I like, and you know how I like it."

She clasped her hands in a silent prayer. "I just need a little more time."

"I've had enough of your games, Priscilla Lee."

"Please."

"Let's see." Wilson reached inside his shirt pocket and pulled out a small, brown, distressed leather-bound book. He cracked open the spine and then licked his forefinger to turn a page or two.

Lilly looked away in disgust. Her stomach churned each time his drool-covered finger kissed the page. "Wh–what's that?" she stammered.

"Priscilla Lee, you're a smart woman. Where's all that female intuition you girls used to brag about back in the day, huh? Take a wild guess."

"I have no idea."

"Sure you do," he insisted. "Just say it."

She couldn't bring herself to think it, let alone say it. She let out a sigh. "Madam Magnolia's little black book?"

"See, I knew you knew. Now, let me spell it out for you. I'm giving you two more weeks. If your daughter is not mine by then, I'm sending a copy of this book to your church. And you know how in the Bible Jesus' words are highlighted in red? I'll make sure all your bedside transactions are highlighted in red, too. Oh, and change your locks."

"Why?"

"You'll see. Is she a virgin?" he asked.

"Of course," she insisted.

"She better be."

"Do I get a bonus?"

"You mean like a finder's fee?"

"Yeah."

"Oh, you'll get your reward."

Free money was sweet money, no matter the source. Always had been, always would be. Lilly stood in line behind Alejandra Katz and her three young children as they checked out groceries in the supermarket. Her dirty blonde hair and tired eyes looked familiar, from church maybe. Lilly couldn't be sure.

Alejandra was so distracted by her bad-assed toddler that she didn't feel the twenty-dollar bill slipping from her grasp. "Elliott, Mommy said get down. Now."

She didn't notice when the bill hit the floor. Lilly did. Slowly, she covered it with her foot and waited.

The exhausted mom opened her wallet and began counting money for the cashier. She was twelve dollars and eighty-seven cents short. She checked her pockets.

"Wait a minute, I know I had another twenty. Maya, Nicholas, have you been in Mommy's purse again?"

"No," they said in concert, shaking their heads.

She rummaged through her purse and scrounged up another four dollars and three cents. "This is crazy. I know I had another twenty." She glanced in Lilly's direction.

Lilly shook her head, mumbling under her breath. "I got a bus to catch. This don't make no kinda sense."

Getting flustered, she instructed the cashier to remove the cereal and juice boxes from her total.

"No, Mommy no," the kids pleaded.

"Mommy'll get them next time." She snatched up her bags along with the toddler and headed for the door. The two older children trailed behind.

Lilly waited until the family left before discreetly sliding the twenty into her territory. Lilly's electric slide. She played her numbers that night and turned a single bill into a wad. How she loved that electric slide.

Hours later, Wilson's words resurfaced in her mind. He meant business. She had nearly died bringing Tootsie into the world thirty-five years ago, she remembered sourly. Once again, Tootsie held the power to make or break her.

Holding onto the couch for support, Lilly slid down to her knees, sending up a fully loaded prayer to God. Having banked mega prayers over the years, her credit with God was good. No, excellent. He had delivered her from many a jam. This time would be no different. She had to convince Tootsie that marrying Wilson was the smartest thing she could do.

Lilly opened her eyes and pulled herself back up onto her feet. She'd prepare Tootsie's favorite meal. Tootsie was truly her mother's daughter—food always flipped her switch. Apparently, that hadn't skipped a generation. A big pot of greens and smothered pork chops—for starters—should do the trick.

Two hours later, Lilly was putting the finishing touches on dinner. Yet while she was cooking, her mind drifted back to another lifetime. She was living once again in sin. In a daze, she reached up into the cupboard for a bowl for the hot buttermilk biscuits. Suddenly feeling dizzy, she placed the bowl on the counter and grabbed a nearby chair to steady herself.

She remembered so vividly being back in Alabama at Madam Magnolia's whorehouse. The next time, she was more careful with her stash. She had come too close, she recalled, to blow it again.

Priscilla Lee's number-one john that time around was a preacher who only wanted to talk. Time was money. He paid her regardless. She had lucked up. Their first time together, he prepaid for her services for the entire week. She loved that he didn't even attempt physical contact. All Reverend Johnson wanted to do was talk about an old church member, and for some reason, Priscilla Lee reminded him of this Beatrice, from her widow's peak and square-shaped face to her full lips and tall, knock-kneed frame. He said he did a double-take when he first laid eyes on her.

Priscilla Lee learned all about Beatrice that night. New to town, Beatrice had been a grocery store cashier whose husband got drunk and beat her every Saturday night. Still, she managed to attend church every Sunday morning, bruises and all. She had no friends, and her husband made sure it stayed that way. One Sunday morning, she slipped a "please help me" note in with her offering. The congregation never saw or heard from Beatrice again. Beatrice's face haunted Reverend Johnson, and he carried that note—along with her obituary—in his wallet as a reminder of his Christian duties.

Priscilla Lee told him that it wasn't his fault, but he wouldn't hear it. When he was all talked out, he stood to leave.

"Will I see you again?"

"It's best if we didn't, but thank you for listening. You understand, don't you?"

Priscilla Lee spent the next few nights on her back, cursing every rancid whiff her nostrils sucked in. She was pondering her options over a Danish and a cup of peppermint tea at the local coffee shop as Reverend Johnson and his wife walked in. He spotted her, too. Their eyes locked and then lowered. She took another sip. She stood and slowly turned, giving him one last chance to process all the possibilities. His eyes followed hers on the way out, confirming a lingering interest.

Lilly could never escape the repercussions of the night she and Reverend Johnson took their tryst to the next level. With her freshly dyed scarlet red curls and matching five-inch nails, Priscilla Lee had run into the reverend and his missus at a local drugstore. She cornered him in the razor blade aisle.

"Hey, Rev." She smiled, a cigarette dangling from her scarlet lips.

"Priscilla Lee, what are you doing here?" he asked, startled.

"Looking for you."

"My wife's in the next aisle. I can't be seen with you."
He started to slide away.

"What do you mean you can't be seen with me?"

"Ssshhh, lower your voice." He looked around.

"Here's the deal," she said, talking fast. "And feel free
to quote me. I am sick of the dick. I'm retiring. So, either
you find something respectable for me to do, or I'll tell
your wife all about those naughty nights at Madam
Magnolia's."

"But nothing happened," he whispered.

"Your word against mine." She shimmied her breasts
before reaching inside her brassiere for a book of matches.
"Now, who do you think she'll believe?"

A week later and with her brunette-colored hair neatly
pulled back into a bun, Priscilla Lee became gainfully
employed as the new housekeeper of Reverend Isaac
and Mrs. Mallory Johnson. She worked six days and
had Sundays off. The first night, she made three-cheese
macaroni and cheese, green beans, and roast chicken.
She was off to a good start. Priscilla Lee 's domestic skills
were challenged, but at least her days of making a living
on her back were over.

Just when her short and stubby hands had the household routine down pat, the childless couple brought home
a stray cat. Mrs. Johnson named him Butter. Priscilla Lee
oohed and aahed right along with them, but when no one
was watching, she'd pinch Butter's behind.

That wasn't the main drawback, though. Mrs. Johnson
had her working from sunrise well into the night. Her
only freedom was in her dreams—until Rev. Johnson
spoiled even those, scratching on her bedroom door one
night until she let him in. Wanting more than conversation, he was as quiet as a kitten licking ice. He crawled
back into his wife's bed just before dawn.

***

The missus couldn't get enough of Priscilla Lee's extra cheesy omelets and home fries. "I swear, your cooking is getting better and better."

"Mallory, I told you about swearing," he reminded her.

She looked up into the heavens. "Sorry, God." She continued, "Priscilla Lee, some man will be lucky to have you. Isn't that right, dear?"

"Amen," Reverend Johnson agreed.

"Do you have a boyfriend?" Mrs. Johnson asked, scooping up some more home fries.

"Mallory, leave the girl alone. Stop prying." The reverend buttered his toast.

"Every girl needs a husband. There's got to be a nice young man at church we can fix her up with," Mrs. Johnson insisted.

"I don't have time for a husband," Priscilla Lee admitted.

"You just haven't found the right one."

Priscilla Lee watched Butter slink across the room like a king, and her resentment built. She gagged every time she cleaned his litter box, every time she peeled cat fur from her clothing.

"Priscilla Lee," Mrs. Johnson began. "You must've been a mouse in a past life."

"Why?"

"Because you love cheese and hate cats."

"Mrs. Watson, I don't hate cats," Priscilla Lee insisted.

"Of course not, only Butter."

Priscilla Lee folded and ironed four loads of laundry while Butter cuddled with Mrs. Johnson. When he had had enough, he went out for some air.

"Butter, Butter," Mrs. Johnson called. She looked around. "Have you seen Butter?"

"He went out for some air. He'll be back."

Butter never came back.

"Isaac, I'm pregnant," Priscilla Lee whispered to the reverend one night after his wife had gone to bed.

"Are you sure?"

"Positive. I'm three months along."

"Dear God." He shook his head.

"What are we gonna do?"

"I'll think of something. Get some rest."

"Priscilla Lee, you're gaining weight," Mrs. Johnson joked days later. "If I didn't know better, I'd think you were pregnant."

"Not me," Priscilla Lee insisted. "Too much macaroni and cheese."

"Honey, I know it's good, but put the fork down," she warned. "'Cause once you lose that girlish figure, it never comes back."

A week before Christmas, Priscilla Lee gave birth to a beautiful baby girl. The Reverend and Mrs. Johnson visited her in the maternity ward.

"That's some mac-n-cheese." Mrs. Johnson laughed. "Has the father seen the baby yet?"

"No, not yet." She eased back in bed. "He's out of town on business right now. When he gets back next week, we're getting married."

"That's wonderful." Mrs. Johnson beamed. "Does he attend church?"

Priscilla Lee bit her lip. "When he can."

"Well, feel free to stay with us for as long as you need to." Mrs. Johnson brightened when the nurses returned with the baby.

"Mrs. Johnson, thank you so much."

Baby Shelby settled into Priscilla Lee's tiny bedroom at the Johnsons', her crib just inches from her mother's bed. One night, after Mrs. Johnson went to bed, Isaac scratched on Priscilla Lee's door.

"I can't stay long," he told her after closing the door. "I just came by to say good night to my daughter." His eyes filled with tears. "It feels so good to have a baby in the house. Thank you. She's beautiful."

Priscilla Lee wiped away a tear, too. "You better go."

Isaac blew them both kisses. "See you tomorrow."

By Valentine's Day, Priscilla Lee's boyfriend had still not returned. Little Shelby was growing like a tadpole. Between working all day for the missus and keeping up with the baby, Priscilla Lee could barely see straight.

She got the baby to bed and drifted off to sleep herself, vaguely aware of the faint sounds of Reverend Johnson and the missus arguing in the background. She woke up refreshed, thankful that Shelby had slept through another night.

Priscilla Lee got up and reached into the crib for Shelby. The infant wasn't there. *Where's my baby?* She ran into the kitchen, the living room, and then the dining room before she barged into the Johnsons' bedroom. The entire house was empty. The closets were cleaned out. She peered through the window. The car was gone.

Numb, Priscilla Lee sat pinned to the sofa until the next morning, her motionless body a mere shell for her fluttering heart. She waited for a month. They didn't return. She never saw Shelby again. The next day, she boarded a Greyhound for New York.

Chapter 16

"Can you believe our nine-year anniversary is coming up?" Sable asked Price over breakfast one morning.

"Seems like only yesterday you were pinning new money inside your underwear," he joked.

"Stop it. You'll never let me live that down." She laughed as she took another sip of coffee. "Chantal wants to throw us a party at church."

He took a long swig of orange juice and then answered, "I guess that's one way of getting me back in church."

"I can't believe I'm letting you talk me into this." Price shook his head at Sable as he adjusted his tie.

"Relax. I promise you'll have a good time."

He kissed her on the nape of her neck, then zipped up the last inch. "All set, Mrs. Galore?"

"Yep," she agreed.

The party was in full swing by the time Price and Sable arrived. Price had to admit that the event planner Chantel hired had done one helluva job decorating, and the caterers weren't half bad either. Too bad alcohol wasn't on the menu.

Price checked out the church crowd as he went to get him and Sable another glass of Coke. He knew he should have brought his flask. Sable would probably have a fit if he went out to his car to get it.

Price had been eyeing a suited-down brother standing on the far side of the room all night. It wasn't just the break in his pants that Price found annoying. He didn't appreciate the way he was in his wife's mouth every time Price looked up, leaving a bad taste in his own.

"Congratulations on nine years," the brown-suited man said, rolling up on him while Sable was in the ladies' lounge.

"Thanks. And you are?" Price asked.

"Adonis. Adonis Watson." He extended a hand that Price didn't shake. "So, what's the secret to staying happily married?"

"Just have to find the right wife," Price told him.

"And that's one high-maintenance wife you got there."

"Well, you're not the one maintaining her." Price looked him over before walking away. He wasn't about to let this checkerboard-toting thug take his queen.

David and Sable managed to slip away from the celebration and were alone in his office. He walked around to the front of his desk and pulled her toward him.

"Sable, I cannot get you out of my mind. Lord knows I've tried. I smell your scent on my fingers. I taste you on the tip of my tongue. You're still purring in my ears."

"David, don't."

"Stop being so coy. You're gonna make me lose my mind," he whispered. David curled her fingers around his erection.

"We can't. Not here"

"You're such a tease."

She blinked in slow motion and swallowed hard. A furtive look came across her face. "Is the door locked?"

"Not yet."

"This is crazy." It took a second for her to pull away. "I shouldn't be in here."

"But you are." He trailed kisses down her neck.

"Yes, but I don't have to stay." She made it to the door before he rear-ended her.

He pinned her against the frame with his body, wrapping his arms around her middle. He locked the office door.

She eased her head back, resting it on his shoulder. "Looks like I'm between a rock and a hard place. Again."

She turned around, and their lips met as his hand slid up her thigh. "Lucky me."

Chapter 17

The first delivery of red roses arrived a bit past noon, taking Tootsie's breath away. Three hours later, a bouquet of yellow roses graced her door, only to be followed by more red roses that evening. In between were deliveries of chocolate-covered strawberries, coconuts, and bananas. There were no cards.

"My baby is finally getting what she deserves." Lilly gushed over dinner. "How do you feel?"

Tootsie giggled with glee. "Like a princess. Who do you think they're from?"

"This is just the beginning. The man has more money than God. Give him a chance."

As if on cue, a single red rose was delivered with a note.

Let's meet tomorrow night at Pretty Titi's Cafe.
Love will be waiting.

Love couldn't tell time. Tootsie looked up, and their eyes met. Adonis smiled, making his way across the floor.

Dismissing him with her hand, she shook her head. "Don't."

"You're kidding, right?"

"Adonis, I'm only going to say this once. You gotta go."

"Looking good, baby girl. I thought it was all for me. Who's it for?"

"Someone you will never be—a big spender who isn't afraid to put his wallet where his heart is."

"Tootsie, my wife stopped by the night of the Comedy Crew show totally unannounced. Anyway, one thing led to another, and I finally agreed to give her a divorce. I pawned my wedding band and headed for the florist. Did you like the roses, Tootsie?"

Her eyes widened. "You're my Prince Charming?"

"Disappointed?"

"Relieved."

He reached for her hands, squeezing their pudginess. "Let's get outta here."

Hours later Tootsie floated into Adonis's third-floor walk-up, winded but more euphoric than ever. She glanced around the typical bachelor's crib as she sat all ladylike in her royal blue dress. There were two closed doors. Which would she choose: the bedroom or the bath? She could keep it clean or play it dirty.

Adonis was waiting for an answer. His eyes twinkled.

"I'm sorry. What were you saying?"

"Can I get you anything?" he repeated.

"No, I'm good."

He joined her on the couch, placing both of her feet in his lap. Then he unbuckled and removed her sandals. She closed her eyes as he began a massage, applying just the right amount of pressure underneath the balls of her feet. He slid Tootsie's big toe into his mouth, sinking her farther into the cushions. Just like that, another cherry . . . popped.

She welcomed Adonis's mouth on hers, the sudden warmth in her loins rising. His fingers gently rubbed the fabric covering her breasts until they budded.

"I'd marry you tomorrow if I could," Adonis said.

"For real?"

He kissed her hands. "In a heartbeat. It's crazy, but spiritually I feel like you're already my wife."

"That's beautiful." She blushed.

"Promise me you'll wait until I'm a free man." He searched her eyes.

"I will."

He smiled, losing her in his dimples. "Not only are you the sexiest woman alive, but you've made me the happiest man alive."

Adonis grabbed his crotch. "Can he have a rub?"

"Okay, but make it a good one."

He did.

The next morning, as the final trail of blood trickled down her thigh and she showered away the last vestiges of her smashed cherry, Tootsie hugged herself and smiled. She and Adonis were in love. This was what all the songs were about. She closed her eyes and relived every detail of their night together. They had only just begun.

He had business to take care of that afternoon, but she was seeing him later that night. She couldn't wait.

But she did. She waited a week for a call that never came. Voicemail after voicemail went unanswered.

Damn, something was wrong. Their love was too strong for games. Maybe he was bleeding to death on the side of the road, or maybe he'd slipped in the shower. Tootsie called the local hospitals. He was either dead, or he was going to be. She camped outside his apartment until she spotted his next-door neighbor. The neighbor told her that Adonis had packed up and left days ago. *What the fuck?*

He used her. She had given her all for nothing. Tootsie blew up his phone all the way home, wishing some cop would pull her over and give her a ticket for using a handheld device while driving. The fury continued once she got in, and she called him once every hour on the hour, until finally he blocked her number. Tootsie threw her phone across the room, shattering it into a dozen pieces. She was through with his broke ass.

"Okay, Mama, I'll do it," Tootsie agreed over breakfast the next morning. "I'll marry Wilson." She bit her lip. A reason, a season, or a lifetime. Adonis had entered her life to smash her cherry. Nothing more, nothing less. He had served his purpose. End of story. Time to move on.

Lilly let out a sigh from deep within. "Oh, Tootsie, you've made me so happy. I'll finally be the mother of the bride. And you, my precious daughter, will be the ultimate lady of leisure—sleeping till noon, shopping all day, endless trips to the hair salon, weekends at the spa," she gushed. "This is the smartest decision you have ever made. No more gingivitis for you. Have you set the date? There's so much to do. And don't forget to go online and order my sanctified brown foundation. I'm getting low."

"I won't, Mama." Tootsie tried to summon up some excitement. "Too bad I can't have a lavish wedding."

"Hmmph, and why not?"

"Thanks, but no thanks. Be glad I'm agreeing to marry him. Let's not push it. A justice of the peace will be fine."

"Are you sure, daughter?"

"Am I sure?" She didn't tell her mother what she really thought. "He's no Prince Charming, but I can still create my happily ever after."

"Now you're talking."

Lilly couldn't wait to share the good news with Wilson. Her daughter was ready and waiting for him to pop the question. She invited him over for coffee and dessert that night so that the two could officially meet. Everything had to be just right. She unpacked her good dishes, the ones reserved for special occasions. If her daughter's engagement wasn't a special occasion, Lilly didn't know what was. She even stopped by the bakery to pick up Tootsie's favorite triple chocolate blackout cake—and a little something for herself—on the way home from playing her numbers. She didn't hit that day, but the two butterscotch pies she sucked down for lunch helped her recover—until she spent the rest of the afternoon glued to the commode. *Damn bakery.*

Completely drained of her energy, Lilly retired to her bedroom and took a long nap. Then, she ran herself a hot bubble bath, dipping her big toe in the Avon-scented water before taking a long soak. At last, she checked the clock. Wilson would arrive in less than half an hour, and she had to get dressed. She lotioned down and baby powdered up before slipping into one of her dressier tents, topping it off with a pair of gold-tone chandelier earrings that she saved for special occasions. She gazed at her reflection in the mirror. She liked what she saw.

"Tootsie?" Lilly knocked on her bedroom door before entering. She thought she had heard her come home. No sign of Tootsie there. She headed down to the kitchen, thinking she was probably stuffing her face. Nope, not there either. Lilly checked her watch. Wilson would be arriving any minute.

Where the heck is that child? She'd be late for her own funeral.

A sudden bout of wedding jitters had landed Tootsie at the hair salon for a fresh cut. "Wait a minute. What do you mean he's gone?" she asked Lilly as she returned home. "He couldn't wait a few minutes for his bride-to-be to arrive? Hasn't he ever heard of someone being fashionably late?"

"Look, daughter, there's nothing fashionable about being two hours late." Lilly began to remove her chandelier earrings. "I told you to be home by seven."

Tootsie rolled her eyes up toward the stratosphere. "My watch stopped, okay?"

"No, it's not okay. You don't know how awkward a situation you've put me in." Lilly slid the salt-and-pepper bun off the back of her head and smoothed back her peak.

"Well, can you at least talk to him?"

"For both of our sakes, I hope so."

Lilly gave Wilson a few days to cool off before contacting him. As she had expected, he refused to answer or return her calls. One day, he had the audacity to hang up on her in mid-sentence. She got the message loud and clear. He called the shots—not her. She gave him space and stopped calling.

Two weeks later, he graced her with a phone call. He talked. She listened. Her chances were up. Her fate was out of her hands, and so was the copy of Madam Magnolia's little black book. As of yesterday, it was en route to the Church of the One Way, courtesy of next day delivery.

Lilly checked her watch, praying she had enough time to intercept the package before it landed in the hands of Sister Doolittle. She didn't have time to listen to any more of Wilson's threats. She dropped the phone and took off running as best she could up the stairs to change clothes. She snatched her purse from the hall closet doorknob and then turned back for Silver, her tiny, shiny revolver.

Huffing and puffing, she boarded the bus, convinced that she was having a heart attack. Still, reputation trumped health. A few passengers turned around to watch as she maneuvered her way to the rear. She plopped down in the last available seat.

After what seemed like three eternities, Lilly exited the bus and began the walk to One Way. The walk that ordinarily took her ten minutes only took six that morning. She almost smiled. If her sides weren't hurting so, it would be funny.

Was that the mailman's truck in the distance? Lilly narrowed her gaze to get a better look. Yep, it was him. She used the last ounce of energy she had to walk that last half block. She reached the church just as the mailman sped off. She was surprised her heart hadn't sped off too. With the help of the railing, she dragged herself up the church stairs one step at a time, catching her breath as she reached the top.

It was quiet and dark inside, and Sister Doolittle was nowhere in sight. She had to think fast. Where would the mail be? She headed straight for the back office and knocked on the door. No answer. The door was locked. Lilly slid a bobby pin out of her bun, quickly jimmied the lock open, and quietly let herself in. The mail sat in a pile on the desk, waiting to get into her hands. She breathed a sigh of relief as she headed toward the desk. Just as she reached for the only parcel on the desk, her deeds came to light.

Someone flipped the damn switch. "What are you doing here?"

Lilly spun around. Sister Doolittle was staring at her like a red hawk.

Lilly grabbed the package off the desk. "Stay out of this, Doolittle."

"Thief! I knew you were a thief!" Sister Doolittle raised her voice. With her Island accent, it sounded like she was calling her a *teef.* "Give me the package, nuh." Sister Doolittle tried to pry it from Lilly's hands.

"No, I will not," Lilly insisted, clutching the package even tighter.

Sister Doolittle finally kicked her in the calf with her pointy-toe kitten-heels, and Lilly buckled over in pain, letting go of the package.

"Ouch!" she yelled.

Sister Doolittle spat in her face. "Illy White, me never like you no how. Never."

"You're gonna pay for this, Doolittle." Blind with rage, Lilly wrapped her hands around Sister Doolittle's neck, and Sister Doolittle started to gurgle as she reached for an envelope opener on the desk. She stabbed Lilly's hand, drawing blood.

"And you call yourself a . . . a . . . missionary. Me never like you no how."

"Every thirty-six minutes someone goes down. Wanna be next?" Lilly aimed Silver at Doolittle's chest.

Sister Doolittle dropped to her knees, begging the smiling missionary not to shoot her. Her eyes filled with tears as she began reciting the Lord's Prayer.

"Our Father, which aren't in Heaven . . ."

"Either He is or He ain't." Lilly laughed so hard her bladder cried. "Get your ass up before I send you there."

She did as she was told. Stunned, she grabbed a few tissues from the box on the desk and blew her nose.

Lilly turned serious as she scooped up the package, making certain that it was Wilson's. "Now, I'm taking this package, understand?"

Sister Doolittle nodded, too scared to speak.

"Good girl. Now, if I so much as suspect that you've breathed a word about me, this package, or what happened here today, me and my little friend will be back to finish the job. You got that?"

Sister Doolittle nodded again.

"You know, I'm getting old. I can't hear you." Lilly cupped her ear.

"Yes, Missionary White." Sister Doolittle was obedient.

"Don't make me hop on my broom," Lilly warned. "Now, get back to work. Jesus is waiting."

After walking in the house, the first thing Lilly did was rip open the package. The little black book was now hers. She allowed the tears to flow as she thumbed through it, line by line, reliving some of the most degrading moments of her life. She went down to the basement and tossed it in a small barrel and lit a match. She watched as Madam Magnolia's little black book was eaten up in flames. Thankful that her past was now behind her, she headed back upstairs.

"Mama." Tootsie shook her head. "I need a job."

Lilly was beaming as she entered the kitchen. "Now, Tootsie, Mama has good news. Wilson has agreed to give us—I mean, you—one last chance. Don't blow it this time."

"I won't, Mama," Tootsie agreed over a bowl of piping hot chili. She crushed a handful of crackers to add to the mix. "So, when are we getting together?"

"He'll be here any minute."

Tootsie looked horrified. "Oh, Mama, I still need time to wrap my mind around him. What's the rush?"

"I can't run the risk of you standing him up again. Come on now, Tootsie. Just think of him as a paycheck for life."

"Well, let me at least go upstairs and freshen up." She sucked down the rest of the chili and put her bowl in the sink.

Twenty minutes later, Tootsie returned, ready to formally meet her soon-to-be husband. Underneath her capri pants and babydoll top, she was Spanxed down.

Lilly rolled her eyes in disgust. "Couldn't you find anything that doesn't make you look like a deluxe entertainment center?"

"Now, Mama, you know I've been big-boned since I was little," Tootsie shot back as she sat down on the sofa and tried crossing her legs.

"Don't, daughter." Lilly shook her head, closing her eyes. "Not a good look."

The peal of the doorbell startled them both. Tootsie sat up straight while Lilly smoothed down her bun.

"Wait a minute, Mama." Tootsie struggled to her feet. "I wanna make an entrance." She nearly tripped over the ottoman as she scurried off to the kitchen.

"That's right, daughter. Go make your grand entrance." Lilly chuckled as she headed toward the door. She was all smiles as she swung it wide open.

"Wilson, it's nice to see you again."

He was in no mood for false pleasantries. "I called your pastor the other day."

"Why would you do that?" She took his hat and coat.

"Seems like he never got the package I sent him."

"Really?" She closed the closet door and turned to face him.

"It takes a real lowlife to steal from a church. There's got to be a special hot spot in Hell for someone like that."

She wasn't giving away a thing. "I can only imagine."

"I bet you can. Anyway, she'll get hers." He took a seat on the couch, while Lilly sat across from him on the recliner.

"What makes you think it's a she?"

"Male intuition. Anyway, that was just a photocopy. You don't think I'd part with Madam Magnolia's real little black book for free, now, do you?"

Lilly shifted gears instantly. "Wilson, you remember my daughter, Tootsie."

"Hello," she said simply.

Tootsie didn't flinch, Lilly was pleased to see. Instead, she willed Tootsie to focus on the life she had always imagined for herself.

Lilly excused herself, leaving the two alone to plan their future.

Tootsie couldn't help but notice the way Wilson's eyes popped as she sat next to him on the couch.

Finally, Wilson spoke. "I know we only met for a brief moment, but you look better than ever."

Tootsie looked him over from head to toe in one quick sweep. His pants were just short enough to be annoying. "Cut the bull. What's in this deal for me?"

"You mean besides being Mrs. Wilson Storm?"

"Yeah, right. That and three dollars will get me on the bus. Exactly."

"What's your asking price?" he said bluntly.

"My asking price?" she repeated.

"Everyone has one."

"Well, fifty thousand dollars for starters."

"Done."

"And a weekly allowance," she continued.

"That goes without saying, unless . . ."

"Unless what?" she asked, turning toward him.

"Unless you're not a virgin. Are you?"

"Of course," she said simply. "My cherry's been marinating for some time. It may take all night to pop."

"Guess we got ourselves a deal."

Three weeks later, dressed in white from head to toe, a marshmallow-esque Tootsie became Mrs. Wilson Storm before a Kew Gardens justice of the peace, as her mother and a courtroom full of couples looked on. Afterward, they went to Applebees for lunch. *Cheap bastard.*

Tootsie beamed as much as could be expected under the circumstances. She overlooked her husband's black suit and white socks, preferring instead to concentrate on the cha-ching of her hefty allowance each time it hit her bank account.

A lip-glossed, sanctified brown-wearing Lilly leaned into Tootsie as Wilson headed for the men's room. "Daughter, you did the right thing. Mama is proud. Be happy."

"Well, Mama," Tootsie began. "If the man don't make me happy, I'm sure his money will."

Lilly May laughed. "Good girl. So, what will you do on your wedding night?"

"Play the part."

She patted Tootsie tidily on top of her hand. "That's all you gotta do, daughter. Just play the part."

Chapter 18

Adonis had moved right around the corner into another walk-up apartment, but that was on a need-to-know basis. He cut Tootsie loose the night he hit it. Sometimes sticking and moving was best, especially when that fairy tale, virginal twinkle hadn't left their eyes.

He'd spotted her a few times in church, but she hadn't caught him. To his surprise, she sported a gold wedding band and a geriatric spouse. Maybe it was safe to unblock her number.

Only one thing kept him coming back to her church's morning worship service: Sable Galore. From the moment he had met Sable at her anniversary party, she had Mr. Happy up nights. She would be the crème de la crème of the M&Ms. She was the total package. Their paths would cross again—accidentally on purpose.

Her husband had too much arrogance pumping through his veins. According to the Greek mythology that Adonis had studied in prison, it was called hubris. Price thought he was a god. Adonis would make Sable the centerpiece of his book, cutting Price down to the quick. Like the nuns had taught him, pride cometh before a fall.

Tootsie called late one night as he was getting ready for bed. He picked up right before she went to voicemail.

"How's it going, Tootsie, or should I say Mrs. Storm?"

"So, you heard. Well, that's Mrs. White-Storm to you." She lost the frosty tone in another instant, though. "Oh, my goodness, Adonis, my life has been mad crazy. Do you hear me? My wedding night was total bullshit. What was I thinking?"

"It's what you were hearing. Cha-ching," he told her knowingly.

"Some things are more important than love."

"Sister, you are preaching to the praise team. But why did you put a ring on it?"

"Financial security. Plain and simple."

Tootsie had depths he had never dreamed of. "Does he make you sleep in the same bed?"

"Every damn night, but I had to tell him, 'Don't be playing no footsies with me. Keep those bad boys to yourself.' And in case you had any doubts, having two balls ain't all it's cracked up to be." She waited for a response that never came. She cut to the chase. "I need to see you."

"I bet you do." He laughed. She was just another married and miserable woman requesting his services. By now, Mr. Happy and his one ball were both swollen. "Why don't we get together, oh, sometime next week?" He hadn't studied street psychology for nothing.

"Are you kidding me? How about tomorrow morning after he leaves the house?"

"I hate to say this, but you made your bed—"

"Fuck you. I know you want some of this," she told him. "Don't even front. I hear you breathing. Your nasty behind is probably jerking off right now."

She wasn't kidding about that. "Okay, meet me in fifteen minutes at the Doubletree Hotel."

"Fifteen minutes? My husband's sleeping in the next room. How am I gonna explain slipping out this time of night?"

"Not my problem. Meet me in fifteen minutes, or Mr. Happy's blocking you again."

"Wait a minute," she began, but he had already hung up.

Wilson Storm waited for Tootsie to disconnect from the living room phone and then hung up softly. He only had a few moments to get dressed and tail his wife.

She led him to the second floor of the Doubletree Hotel. He couldn't believe how easy following her had been. Apparently, this Adonis was waiting inside. She entered the room and quickly closed the door behind her.

Just as he had hoped, in her haste to be fucked, she had forgotten to close the hotel room door all the way. Wilson cracked the door open just in time to see Tootsie slip out of her sundress. Adonis quickly helped her out of her red bra and matching panties. They both stretched out naked on the bed. Wilson couldn't believe it. The sight of his bride being pumped by another man was like porn, giving him a rise and working faster than the little blue pill ever could. Soon his crotch was bursting at the seams. Right there in the darkened hallway, he unzipped his fly and began pleasuring himself, unable to take his eyes off of Adonis ramming his meat into his wife. After they climaxed, he did too.

He ran all the red lights to get home before she did.

Tootsie barely showered in her haste to return home. The house was quiet. No sign of Wilson. She decided she'd take a hot bath before calling it a night. She filled the bath with bubbles and then slid in. The water soothed her, giving her time to relive her guilty midnight pleasure with Adonis. Just because she was married didn't mean she had to stop having fun. Smiling, she dozed off for a few.

Suddenly, she was awakened by the feeling that she was not alone. Tootsie nearly jumped out of her skin at the sight of Wilson standing in the doorway, his erect penis peeking out of his towel. She tried to get up, but he caught her on the bathtub's ledge. She couldn't explain the madness or the crazed look in his eyes that mirrored her own, but in that instant, she knew she wanted her husband, too.

Upping his habit to a pack of cigarettes a day, Adonis spent the next week unloading the manuscript out of his head and onto the page. *Cheat Like a Lady, Snatch Like a Man* had bestseller written all over it, but how to convey that to the world?

He checked the caller ID on his phone. It was the call he had been dreading, his editor Giselle Wolfson.

"Good morning, Giselle. How are you?"

"You tell me," she replied, iciness jumping off her cords.

"Working hard on that manuscript. Real hard. The end is finally in sight," he lied.

"You know, Adonis, I went out on a limb to get you that contract. If you can't deliver . . ."

For a moment, he debated giving her a sample of Mr. Happy to shut her ass up. "I'm wrapping it up as we speak." Another lie. "Let me get back to work. You're wrecking my flow."

"Talk to you later."

"Much later," he agreed before hanging up.

Adonis stared at the same page for nearly half an hour, blinded by the white. Nothing. Maybe he needed some inspiration.

***

Adonis nearly collided with a woman in the produce department as he headed to the deli for more bologna and cheese. Though her smile was familiar, Adonis couldn't quite place her. Not until their paths crossed again in the parking lot did he recall where they had met—at Sable's anniversary party and church.

Adonis immediately locked up his dinner and approached her, slipping between several parked cars in the process. After loading the groceries into the back seat, she had just closed the rear door when Adonis approached her.

"I think I know you," he began.

"I was wondering how long it would take you." Her eyes twinkled. "You were at Sable and Price's anniversary party."

"And you are?"

"Bubbles."

"Nice to finally meet you, Bubbles. I'm Adonis. That was some lovefest, huh?" he asked, referring to Sable and Price.

"Yeah, she must have a honey drip between her legs, 'cause Price treats her like a damn queen," she said bitterly. "They looked like Ken and Barbie working the room until you had that sidebar with Price. What was that all about anyway?"

"Price still has a beef with me. Me and Sable used to kick it back in the day," he lied.

Bubbles' mouth dropped upon hearing Adonis's embellishment. "I had no idea."

"Sometimes you just wanna do 'em and dump 'em."

"You dumped Sable?" Her eyes lit up. "That's what I'm talkin' about."

Chapter 19

"We need to talk," Tootsie told her husband as she threw back another bourbon.

"About what?"

"That night you jammed me up in the tub."

"You need to go easy on that stuff. Hell, it ain't even noon yet."

She ignored him, lighting up a cigarette and welcoming more of the brown liquid. With just the right amount of burn, it took control, hitting the back of her throat.

"What's there to talk about? We both liked it," he said.

"I married you for business, not pleasure. Keep it in your pants."

"Can't I shower you with the best of both worlds?"

"As if you could."

"Well, I didn't do too bad the other night."

"Beginner's luck," she shot back.

"Ya think?"

To prove her point, Tootsie opened her robe and wrapped Wilson in her voluptuousness. She waited for a response that never came.

"Like I said, beginner's luck."

Wilson reached for the half-empty bourbon bottle and poured himself a drink. "I forgot how new you are to the game. There are so many avenues to desire."

She chuckled. "Avenues to desire? What's that, the title of some damn book you're writing?"

"You have no idea how a little creativity on your part could keep me at a full tank. And I'm not talking about that new cherry red lipstick you like to pop either."

"Wilson, puhleez. Ain't that much Viagra in the world. Who you kiddin'?"

Grinning with his oversized teeth, he swirled the bourbon around the glass before taking another sip. "Not so young, but oh, so naïve. Viagra had nothing to do with your orgasms. Hell, mine either."

"My bad. Ain't that much Cialis in the world."

"But there's plenty of you," he reminded her.

"Look, this ain't the day." The bathroom scale had registered another six pounds since last week.

"Relax. There's a hot new game in town. You want in?"

Tootsie rolled her eyes to the moon. "Whatever your nasty little behind is selling, I'm not interested."

"Well, you were sure eating it up that night."

"Trust me, it won't happen again."

"It could and it should," he shot back. "I am your husband, remember? And I won't pressure you into anything you don't want, okay?"

"Go on."

"That night you slipped out after midnight . . ." he began.

She immediately grew tense. "I just needed some air."

"Is that what you're calling it? Anyway, I followed you. Imagine my surprise when I saw my recently deflowered new bride and what's his name? Adonis? Screwing like a couple of alley cats in that hotel room. It drove me nuts."

She opted for attitude to see her through. "Hmmph, don't get it twisted. Just because we're married doesn't mean you know how to put a ring on it. Now, Adonis? That man's name is written all over my cookie jar."

Wilson jumped in her face. "Is that right?"

The scent of Bengay hit her nostrils. "Yeah, that's right. Look, I promised you my hand in marriage. Nothing else."

"Let's both benefit from your liberated coochie."

Was he for real? She stood and took one last sip of her drink. "Hair appointment, gotta go."

"Hear me out."

"Five seconds, Wilson."

He returned to the chair. "Why don't I take you shopping for whatever you heart desires?"

"Go on."

"We go out on the town, and you pick any man you want. We'll call it the pick-and-pay game night. I'll slip him a few bills, and he's yours for the night. Just let me watch from the closet."

She opened her mouth, but nothing came out. She definitely wasn't in Kansas anymore.

"I know. Give it some thought," he told her. "We'll talk later."

Looking like she had just stepped off a runway for bootylicious plus-size models, Tootsie squeezed into a booth opposite her husband at Pink Ice, one of Long Island's newest hotspots. Close enough to Queens yet tucked away deep enough in Nassau County, the club offered the perfect touch of anonymity and trend for the sexually adventurous couple. Tootsie didn't know who was crazier: Wilson for having the audacity to suggest something so ludicrous, or her for trying to make up for lost dick years. Were a few more dollar bills and baubles worth an express ride to hell?

The newly purchased emerald green choker adorning her throat clinched it. She was being groomed for whoredom. If Lilly knew that not only was Wilson pimping her out, but that she was going along with his program, who would she crucify first?

Tootsie stroked the stones around her neck as she scanned the club once more. No one hit her sweet spot. Maybe she'd have better luck with the food.

A waitress came to take their orders, vanishing soon afterward. Wilson's scowl said it all as he checked his watch in the semi-darkness. Girlfriend had just blown her tip. Even after a trip to the infamously crowded ladies' lounge, Tootsie beat the appetizers to the table. She slipped out of her shoes to relieve the pressure on her corns, but to no avail.

Maybe she and Wilson should leave. Just as she wiggled into her pumps, dinner arrived. Choosing food over discomfort, Tootsie inhaled the smothered chicken and cabbage.

The last morsel had hit her palate, and she and Wilson had just requested the dessert menu, when he walked through the door. He sat just a few tables away to their right. Her sweet spot tingled as she glossed over his thick neck and tight physique, then back at the desserts. Torn between him and the promise of sin on a plate, her freshly picked cherry chose him.

Wilson followed Tootsie's gaze, landing on him, too.

"You want Big Papa to get that for you?" he asked, adjusting his tie.

Tootsie dared not speak for fear of furthering her husband's perversion along with her own. Instead, she bit her bottom lip.

"You're the boss."

With a snake-eyed grin and deep pockets, Wilson strolled over to their first victim, apologizing for the intrusion. The prospective john shot Wilson a look of disbelief before his eyes narrowed and settled upon Tootsie. Unwilling to meet his gaze, Tootsie concentrated on the coffee list. His eyes went from Wilson's full-figured wife to Wilson's fuller-figured wallet. Tootsie thanked God she could read lips.

"Ain't rocket science." Wilson pulled out a hundred-dollar bill.

"You wired?" The john's eyes darted around the club as Wilson began peeling off more bills, promising half now and the rest later.

"Okay, ol' man, I'm down."

"Meet me in five in the parking lot." Wilson slipped him a couple of condoms before rejoining his bride.

For the first time that evening, Tootsie and the john's eyes met. And lingered.

"Ready, my sweet?" Wilson sealed the deal with a peck to her cheek.

Tootsie sat numbly in the tub, struggling to wash away all vestiges of that evening at Pink Ice. In the midst of a New York heat wave, she was still frozen. The three had convened in the parking lot. The stranger's eyes slowly swept over Tootsie's in-your-face curves as Wilson did everything short of licking his lips. The next step was all planned. They checked into a room at a nearby hotel and would let nature take its course.

Nature never did. Tootsie bolted before the stranger's clothes hit the floor. She wanted no part of this depravity. Just as she was about to descend into the pits of hell, God snatched her back up, redeeming her once again by His blood.

She'd cabbed it home, only to find that Wilson had beat her there. She and Wilson had had a knock-down, drag-out that night. She was through being a hostage in this masquerade of a marriage. The money wasn't worth the weirdness. She'd go back to work.

Without uttering a word, Tootsie escaped to the spare bedroom to retrieve her packed bag. Kneeling on all fours, she felt around for the handle and pulled her bag out. It was time to go home. Only Wilson stood between her and sweet freedom.

"Where do you think you're going?"

"Get your puny ass out my way." She tugged at a wedding band that would not budge, but then, she was glad about that. Better money in her pocket than thrown in his face.

"Do what you must." He smirked. "You'll be back."

Tootsie hopped in her car and sped off, red lights powerless in her path. She couldn't wait to be swallowed up by her own bed, to wake up to Lilly's home-cooked wonders wafting through the house. She climbed her mother's stoop and slid the key in the door. Her smile evaporated as she jiggled the knob. Nothing. What the hell?

Tootsie rummaged through her purse. She had picked locks before, and she was prepared to do it again. Where the hell were her dental tools? She could use a scaler right about now.

Tootsie phoned her mother from the stoop. It went straight to voicemail. She looked up. Lilly's bedroom lights were still on.

"Mama, it's me. Open the door." She banged on the door. "Mama?"

"Hush your mouth." Lilly had opened the screen, and her ominous presence hovered over Tootsie. "I'm trying to get some sleep. What's wrong with you?"

"I left Wilson, Mama. Let me in."

"You what? Daughter, you must be out your mind. You landed a good man. Go home, Tootsie."

"I am home. He's a pimp, Mama."

"And you're a grown woman, Tootsie. I keep telling you. Marriage is a grown woman's game. You better start acting like it."

Lilly's neighbors' shouts to shut up only made her bang louder. "Open the door, Mama."

"Tootsie, you are disturbing my peace. Go home to your husband, or I will call the cops. Now, good night." Lilly slammed the window shut, and the house went black.

"Total bullshit."

Tootsie tried calling Bubbles. Six rings, and then voice-mail. She sat quietly in the car and gathered her thoughts before redialing Bubbles. This time, it went straight to voicemail.

Tootsie took a cleansing breath before yanking the ruby-red choker from her neck, spewing stones all over the front seat. She palmed her fresh 'do and then started the engine.

There's no place like home . . . There's no place like home.

But where, exactly, was home?

Chapter 20

Adonis had a ten o'clock appointment in Manhattan with his editor. The problem was that his mechanic had promised his car would be ready two days ago, but the part he had ordered hadn't arrived yet.

Adonis raced down the escalator at the Jamaica Long Island Railroad station and slipped on the last step just as the 9:16 train pulled off. Shit, he'd have to wait for the next one. To make matters worse, a mosquito bit him on his right eyelid. Adonis used the extra time to purchase a round-trip ticket from the machine, saving himself a few bucks. His cell phone service was disconnected for non-payment, so he needed every dime he could get.

Finally, Adonis boarded the 9:30, plopping his frame into a backward-facing seat. He'd be in New York in twenty minutes, but that didn't stop him from resting his eyes as the lid began to swell. Scratching made it worse. Winking made him look like a pervert, especially when the woman sitting across from him rolled her eyes and abruptly changed seats.

Don't nobody want your fat ass, lady.

Adonis checked his watch. Giselle was so freaking anal when it came to her schedule. There was no way to tell her he was running late. He drummed his fingers on his thigh.

The train pulled into Penn Station on time. Limited by the crowd, he climbed the stairs one at a time. As he approached street level, sunlight scorched his eyes, forcing him to reach for the sunglasses in his sports jacket's breast pocket. Black men and taxis weren't a Manhattan mix, so he walked to his editor's office.

He was ten minutes late. Chloe Long, Giselle's assistant, was an eyeglass-wearing, chubby-faced, blue-eyed woman sitting behind her desk. The reception area was empty.

"I'm sorry, Mr. Watson, but Giselle will not be able to see you today. Would you like to reschedule? Let's see what's available." She checked the computer for appointment slots.

"No, I'll wait, Chloe." He took a seat on the brown leather sofa.

Half an hour later, Giselle and a client appeared in the doorway. Giselle seemed to be wrapping things up. She glanced over at Adonis in the waiting area. He was hoping to charm Giselle into another advance. The tautness in her jaw said otherwise.

"Okay, Martin." She extended her hand. "Keep me posted."

"We'll talk soon," he agreed, putting his hand in hers.

Adonis stood and approached Giselle. He opened his mouth to speak, but she held up her hand, halting his words.

"You're late. My schedule's tight. You're free to reschedule."

"I know your name's on the letterhead, but come on. All I need is five minutes," he insisted.

"Then you should have been here forty minutes ago," she reminded him, glancing at her watch. "Where's that bestseller I keep hearing about?"

"Not quite finished."

"That's what I thought. Next time, wear a watch."

"I have one."

"Use it." She turned to her assistant. "Chloe, reschedule Mr. Watson."

"Look, don't talk to me out of pocket. I'm not your child."

"Then grow up." Giselle returned to her office, shutting the door behind her.

Chloe bit her lip. "Mr. Watson, when would you like to come back?"

"Anything next week?" He leaned toward her. "You couldn't pay me for your job."

Chloe checked her schedule. "Sorry, but she has an opening week after next. Wednesday at eleven-thirty?"

"That'll be fine," Adonis agreed, his pulse rising.

Chloe printed the confirmation and handed it to him. "See you then, Mr. Watson."

His chest tight, Adonis took the elevator to the lobby. He pounded his fist into the elevator wall, his eyes daring the other riders to say one word. Was he more angry at Giselle or himself?

Once outside, he took a walk up to Times Square to clear his head. Even before noon, the Midtown streets were lively. He passed a homeless man with a horrendously scarred forehead, begging for money. Adonis said a silent prayer and kept moving.

Feeling sweat streaming down his back, he removed his jacket at the crosswalk. He stepped off the curb just as the light turned green, but an eager cabbie roared through the red light, missing him by follicles.

"Bastard," Adonis yelled, punching the hood of the taxi with his fist à la *Midnight Cowboy*. "The light's red, dammit." He shook his head. Everybody was in such a damn hurry.

That reminded him. Giselle was such a bitch. Like her minutes were so important that she couldn't spare five. Who needed her? He did. The inner rage he felt cooled down into the depression that had him in its grip lately. He was down to eight hundred dollars, and he still had rent, food, and his car to worry about. What the hell was he supposed to do? He could really use some help.

Adonis stopped at TGI Friday's, wanting vodka but ordering beer. He nursed it for as long as he could before ordering another. Being poor was one thing, but looking it was another.

After four straight days of rain, the lunchtime crowd, under the spell of a seductive summer sun, flew in, bringing their rowdiness with them. He gulped down his second beer and left.

Hell, maybe he'd hang out in the city and watch Manhattanhenge along Forty-second Street. The perfect summer sunset awed him every time.

Nearing the Marriott, Adonis slowed down and did a double take.

Wait a minute. Is that—? No, it can't be.

"Well, I'll be damned." He grabbed his ball. Pastor Dante was leaving the hotel, linked up with Sable and First Lady Chantel, who was holding hands with Price. Just as they were about to step into a cab at the curb, the pastor pulled her back with one hand and took her into his arms. They kissed hungrily before all four jumped into the waiting cab and sped away.

Damn, the pastor was just another church slick dick, and Dante's *Inferno* never hotter.

Cha-ching. Even without a smartphone, he had the money shot. Stroking his goatee, Adonis thanked his lucky stars for missing the 9:16 train. Time for a bottle-poppin' party night.

"Alejandra, what exactly do you know about Adonis? I mean, really."

"We go way back. Sable, he's not perfect, but a part of me gets him."

"But do you trust him? He's a snake. He'll steal your eyeballs right out of their sockets. Just be careful."

Alejandra's mommy ears perked up. "Elliott's awake. Milk's in the fridge," she reminded her before going to check on him.

Sable opened Alejandra's refrigerator, shocked by what she saw, or more importantly, didn't see. She lightened her coffee and returned the quart to the bare shelf just as Alejandra returned with Elliott clinging to her thigh. She scooped him up and rejoined Sable at the table.

Elliott and Sable played a game of peekaboo before he got cranky and slid from his mother's lap onto the floor. Suddenly fascinated with Sable's ankle bracelet, he wrapped his pudgy fingers around her calf.

"A leg man in the making." Sable laughed.

"Already," she agreed. "Elliott, get from under there. Elliott? Don't you hear Mommy calling you?" She bent down and snatched him up. "Sable, you sure you don't want one? How'd you get through all these years without kids anyway?"

"Just lucky, I guess." Sable shrugged. "Listen, I'm gonna run so Elliott can have you all to himself."

"Okay." She stood and saw Sable to the door.

"Take care, Alejandra. Bye, Elliott." She stroked his hair.

"Buh-bye," Elliott said, blowing her a kiss.

Sable had reached her car before she stopped. She couldn't just leave, not with the refrigerator empty like that. She got Alejandra on the phone.

"What are you doing right now?" she asked.

"Just trying to get something together for Elliott's lunch."

"I'm still here. We're going grocery shopping."

"Sable, no. I'm good."

"I'm giving you five minutes, or I'm coming back up."

"Sable, it's okay. Really."

"Four minutes, Alejandra." Sable disconnected.

Half an hour later, Alejandra and her son maneuvered an ever-growing shopping cart into the supermarket's produce area. "Sable, this is too much," she whispered. "Are you sure you want to do this?"

"Of course. Go shop." She shooed her away. "I have things to get, too. Meet you up front when you're through. Get what you need and have fun."

"Sable, I don't know how I'll ever repay you."

"You don't have to. I can't call myself a child of God and do nothing when you need a little help."

"God bless you, Sable."

"I'm blessed to be a blessing to you. Now, go."

Alejandra did as she was told, but Sable sent her back for more. When she had three shopping carts, beyond what Midnight could ever carry, Sable ordered home delivery.

Alejandra had raved about Pastor Dante's skills, even suggested that Adonis pay him a visit. If she only knew. And he had the nerve to call himself a pastor. Adonis set up an appointment with Pastor Dante. He'd break the ice and then watch him squirm.

They met at the church. His office was free of nosy deacons and snooping missionaries. Awards and certificates riddled the walls, while thick, chocolate brown carpeting cushioned his feet. Pastor Dante sat behind a massive cherry wood desk cluttered with papers. To his right lay a large black leather-bound Bible opened to the ninety-first Psalm. A wedding photo with first lady Chantel graced his left.

"So, Brother Watson, how can I be of service?"

"Well, you know, Pastor," Adonis began, "I believe in God. I read my Bible. Not every day, but as often as I can. And I attend service."

"Sounds like you're doing more than most of my congregation," Pastor Dante said cheerfully.

"But some things I need to have explained," he said, warming to his subject. "Sometimes I think about entering the ministry. I'd be good at it."

"It's not a job. You have to be chosen by God," Pastor Dante reminded him.

He thought about that. "Yeah, I guess it would have to be. I'll take your word, though." Adonis continued, "Now, I've read all about the Garden of Eden and the serpent in the book of Genesis. What I don't get is this: If God formed Adam from the dust of the ground dirt, what makes people think that God's chosen people are white?" He raised his hand to forestall any interruption. "Don't insult my intelligence. Snow is white. Dirt is brown. I went to kindergarten. I know my colors. I know the difference. If Moses' skin turned white from leprosy before returning to its natural color, obviously he wasn't a pale male to begin with, and neither was Jesus."

"I know, Brother Watson, but try not to concentrate on race and skin color. We are more alike than different, and we are all created in His image. God is so awesome that He manifests in as many races, creeds, colors, and ethnicities as there are people. Water, steam, ice—it's all good. We already know history was airbrushed so that all the biblical characters look like the dominant culture. Don't focus on Charlton Heston or Kanye. Focus on Jesus and His love."

Adonis nodded slowly at the pastor's words. "Now, let me ask you another question, Pastor Dante. Do you think clergymen are held to an even higher standard when they sin than, say, laymen?"

"Absolutely."

"Sometimes I think that life is just the same biblical script and characters set on different stages recurring throughout the ages."

"Interesting."

"So, tell me." Adonis leaned forward in his seat. "Which biblical character are you most like?"

"I would say David."

"Wow, David. That's deep. Talk about a complex man."

"My parents named me David because they knew I'd be a man after God's heart."

"David loved the Lord, but that brother was a hot mess. Deception, murder, adultery . . ." His voice trailed off. "Like people at the Marriott. Or at least that's what I've seen."

There was dead silence. In that moment, both men knew. Only a sudden knock at the door defused the room's tension.

Pastor Dante cleared his throat. "Yes?"

"Pastor, the trustees need a quick word with you about Sunday's service."

"I'll be right there, Deacon Greer." Pastor Dante stood. "Excuse me, Brother Watson." Pastor Dante stepped out, leaving the door slightly ajar. Adonis watched him disappear down the hall.

Adonis shot a glance toward the door before eyeing the paperwork on the desk. Jumping up, he rifled through some letters, mostly speaking engagement invitations, copies of old church programs, and a draft of this Sunday's sermon. He snuck another peek down the hall before flipping through the leather-bound Bible in search of God knows what.

He thumbed through the Old Testament. Bookmarking the twentieth chapter of Exodus was a blank check payable to Pastor David Dante, signed by Price Galore, which he quickly pocketed. *What the heck?*

Chapter 21

On Wednesday night, Bubbles rushed home from work to make Hayden's favorite dish—lamb chops, garlic mashed potatoes, asparagus, and garlic bread. She took extra care to prepare the lamb chops just the way he liked them, not too rare. Everything had to be just so, and she was as sweet as could be that evening, careful to avoid his wrath. She piled his plate high with plenty of carbs. He had two helpings before retiring to the living room, where she brought him his iced tea.

Half an hour later, Hayden was out. Bubbles checked her watch. It was only seven thirty, still too early to snatch Sable's trash. She waited a couple more hours and checked on Hayden again. He was normally a light sleeper, but she could tell by his snoring that he'd sleep through the night.

She grabbed her purse and car keys and headed out the door. She breathed in a whiff of pure freedom. Rarely did Hayden allow her to go out alone after dusk. The intoxicating night air would be her confidante, concealing her secret mission.

Smiling, Bubbles started the car and headed for Baldwin Hills. She clicked on the radio, and the soulful R&B carried her through. Caught up in the vibes, she missed her exit. No one was behind her, though, and she reversed for a few feet and detoured onto the ramp. She was in Baldwin Hills in no time.

Bubbles couldn't believe her eyes when she pulled up in front of Sable's house. Comparing it to her own gave her another reason to hate that bitch. Even if she died and went to Heaven, Bubbles doubted if she could ever live in such posh digs.

As effortlessly as she could, Bubbles hopped out of the car, grabbed two trash bags of garbage from in front of the house, hauled them into her late-model Chevy, and sped off. Her heart rate didn't return to normal until she was back on the Belt Parkway.

Once home, she checked on Hayden. He was fast asleep where she had left him on the couch. She let out a sigh and quickly returned to the car. One at a time, Bubbles pulled the trash bags up the front stoop and into the house. When she heard Hayden stir, she grabbed them by their handles and hid them in her coat closet. They'd have to wait for another day.

Another day turned into three. Bubbles couldn't sneak the garbage bags out of the closet if she tried. Hayden came down with a summer cold and camped out on the living room sofa, wrenching her plans. He was so congested that he was spared from the foul odor wafting from the closet. Bubbles wasn't. By the time she finally managed to get to the bags, cartons of half-eaten Chinese take-out and an opened can of evaporated milk nearly made her puke, but the empty bottle of Sable's signature perfume made it all worthwhile. If she started wearing that scent, maybe Price would love her too.

Bubbles put her garbage out later that night, smiling all the way to the curb. Sable wasn't the only one worthy of a $400-per-ounce fragrance, and Bubbles had the funds to prove it. She'd make a hefty withdrawal from her mad money account and give Sable a nice big whiff of her own perfume. She didn't intend to keep the perfume; she just wanted Sable to know that two could play her game.

She rubbed her behind, recalling her last mad money account withdrawal and those damn turquoisey-teal crystal stiletto peep-toe pumps. Next time would be different. She'd be more careful.

Hayden's illness left her climbing the walls. Bubbles schemed madly for an excuse to get out of the house and drive to Roosevelt Field to pick up the fragrance. She had already called Bloomingdale's in Manhattan, and they were temporarily out of stock. As luck would have it, just when Bubbles' patience could last no longer, Hayden was invited to a two-day pastor's anniversary celebration in Jersey. Bubbles feigned a migraine to get out of the trip. She stayed in a darkened bedroom all morning, a wet washcloth covering her forehead, a wastebasket next to her bed to catch the vomit that would never come.

The moment she heard his car drive off, she jumped up and got dressed. Just once, she wanted to know how it felt to be pampered like Sable. She picked up the perfume and then spent the rest of the afternoon at a day spa. She had a deep tissue body massage followed by reflexology and a soothing scalp massage. Afterward, she stopped at Crumbs for a scrumptious red velvet cupcake. She nearly broke the bank, but it turned into one of the most lazy, luscious days she could remember. No wonder the heifer was always smiling.

Her joyride came to a screeching halt as she slammed on the brakes to avoid turning a three-car accident into four. The peal of an approaching siren nixed Bubbles' idea of riding the shoulder to her exit. She crept along, uncertain of which moved faster—her car, or the minute hand on her watch.

She didn't have to wonder for long. Hayden's call confirmed it for her.

"Hello?" She turned down the radio.

"I've been home for over an hour. Where the hell are you?"

"I . . . I ran out to Roosevelt Field to get a few things for your birthday and got caught in a traffic jam," she stammered. Thank God Hayden was too cheap to install GPS on her phone. "There's been a terrible accident on the Belt."

"My birthday's months away," he told her.

"I know, but JCPenney's was having a sale, and—"

"Penney's? That bag better be full, or your ass won't be worth two cents," he warned before disconnecting.

Bubbles was so screwed that it wasn't funny. She checked her watch. It was after ten thirty, and JCPenney had closed over an hour ago. Where the hell was she going to find a crisp new Penney's shopping bag at this hour—even if she was lucky enough to find something to fill it with? Bubbles shook her head as traffic resumed.

As a last-ditch effort, she tried calling Tootsie. *Answer the damn phone.* The call went straight to voicemail. *Hmmph.* Apparently, she was with that wonder-stud husband of hers.

She pulled up in front of the house and sat, unwilling to go in. She had to face the music. What could Hayden do to her for not wanting to spoil his birthday surprise?

To her relief, he did absolutely nothing. He didn't even bring it up when she finally entered their bedroom after eleven. Instead, he greeted her with a loving kiss.

"Boy, I'm a lucky devil having a wife who shops for my birthday gift months in advance." He stood behind her and wrapped his arms around her waist.

"That you are." She smiled, her breathing returning to normal.

"Let's celebrate now."

Bubbles stiffened and prepared for an all-out blowout, but before she had a chance to answer, Hayden reached for her purse on the bed. He tore an even bigger hole in an already shabby comforter. Bubbles lunged forward, attempting to rescue her bag from his clutches. He threw her to the floor, but she got right back up. Bubbles bit him hard on his bicep, drawing blood. He backhanded her, and she hit the floor once more. This time, he sat on her.

Hayden opened the purse. Her wallet, lipstick, keys, cosmetic case, and a pack of gum were all tossed over his shoulder before he turned her purse upside down and shook it vehemently.

Hayden's eyes grew dark as underwear landed in his lap. He unloosened his belt buckle and removed his belt, his eyes never leaving hers. Whistling, he locked the bedroom door and closed the windows. Bubbles' eyes were fixated on the belt. Was she strong enough, she wondered, to wring his neck?

Without saying a word, he removed her clothing, shoes, and underwear. Hayden grabbed the TV remote in order to blast the volume. He grabbed another belt from the closet door handle and tied her wrists together.

"Please, no," she pleaded, backing up.

Hayden was immune to her pleas. "Don't you know that cheaters and beaters don't mix?" He took one step forward, and she, three steps back.

Before Bubbles could react, Hayden swung, and the leather ripped into her flesh. She cringed in pain and absorbed another cut. Bubbles' screams only fueled more rage. The belt stung her again and again. Blood and welts popped up on her back, arms, and legs. Again and again, he skinned her with his wrath, her nakedness still reeling from one hit before another one struck.

She hobbled around the room, tearing down lamps, curtains, anything she could latch onto. With his fingers wrapped around her throat, he maneuvered Bubbles into a corner. She managed to stop his choking death grip by kneeing him in the groin. Then, everything went black.

Chapter 22

"Damn it, Sable. I texted you samples of furs for the holiday collection catalog half an hour ago. You know I'm meeting the Smith brothers tonight. Why didn't you call me back?" Price demanded. The Smith brothers were prospective clients.

"Sorry, baby, I guess I conked out."

"You're always so tired lately. Take some vitamins or something."

Sable made a mental note to see the doctor. She grabbed her phone and sat up in bed. Yawning, she checked out the furs.

"Any of them grab you?"

"The raccoon and definitely that chinchilla."

"And what about the fox?" he asked her.

"Let me get to—" she said, her jaw suddenly dropping. "Ooh, now that's gorgeous."

"You think so?"

"Whaaat? Are you kidding me?"

"Okay." He laughed. "Listen, those Smiths can throw back some gin. Don't wait up."

After he was gone, Sable got a text alert.

Meet me at the Marriott on Lexington.

She texted back: No private hook-ups. Remember?

Another response hit seconds later. Pleeez? You want me to beg for it, don't you?

Even his texts blew her hair back.

We can't!!!

Would he ever let her be? Sable made a decision. She turned off her phone, feeling stronger already.

She stripped, eager for a long, hot shower. The water soothed her before she slipped into a cool cotton night-shirt, readjusted her pillows—and then ended up tossing back and forth between her side of the bed and Price's. Not a good night for sleeping when she ached for so much more. Finally, she turned her phone on. Another text winked.

If you change your mind, I'll be there until midnight.

Sable's eyes shot to the nightstand. It was already past ten. Dare she even think of another night with him? She knew she shouldn't, but she checked the railroad schedule anyway before she lost her nerve. She could be in the city and in his arms before midnight, though she had no business being in either.

Vacillating, Sable rolled over, allowing her gnawing appetite for David to marinate until she was awakened this time by her own orgasm.

She called Price.

"How's it going?"

"They screwed up our reservations. We just sat down to dinner."

"Sounds like it's gonna be a long night."

"Very. Listen, I'll call you later.

"Okay, but can we—" she began. He had already hung up.

It was almost ten thirty. Sable snatched a few condoms from Price's secret stash and was in David's suite barely before the top of the clock.

He picked her up, tossed her over his shoulder, and carried her caveman-style into the bedroom. Then he put her down gently on her own two feet. He removed his shirt and unbuckled his belt. She caught a glimpse of his red boxers before her eyes raced back to his.

He gently kissed her neck and décolletage. "I didn't think you were coming."

"David, we need to talk."

"Okay, let's talk." He unzipped his pants, telling on himself.

She sucked in air. Suddenly, talking was the last thing on her mind. "David, you don't play fair."

He placed her hand around his bulging prize. "Tell that to him."

Her hand lingered longer than it ought to. Finally, she released her grip, and he removed his pants, tossing them over the back of the chair.

He parted her lips, kissing her hard as they both stood. Her tongue slid around and down his chest, his navel, and beyond. Sable's long-held views on right and wrong, good and bad, blurred, morphing into the tiny drops of dew between her thighs. Then she stood and peeled off her clothing, leaving nothing on except her panties. She stripped the bed of its comforter and blanket before easing back onto the crisp white sheets.

"David, you have one last chance to walk out that door and save us both."

With his hands on his hips, David considered what she said, his eyes never leaving hers. "You're right." He turned and got as far as the chair before turning around to face her. He removed his boxers. Sable's panties were off before he hit the sheets. He snatched a foil packet from the nightstand, tore it open with his teeth, and slid the condom on. She barely had time to open her legs before he was inside her, pushing them both into another dimension.

"David, this has got to stop," she panted.

"I know," he agreed. "It has to."

Sable had vowed never again, and yet here she was, opening her playground to him. Sable and David pleasured each other every way imaginable that night. It had to be a sin to cum so many times before dawn. Sable prayed that if they got each other completely out of their system, maybe he could go back to being just her pastor. But each time he made her climax, her prayers grew more faint.

Price's secretary knocked on the door, interrupting his thoughts.

"Mr. Waterburg is here," Selena told him.

"Give me a moment, and then show him in." Price shuffled some paperwork on his desk.

"Sure, Mr. Alexander." She nodded before closing the door behind her.

Price had been on the IRS's radar for quite some time. Paul Waterburg was one of the best, if not the best, tax attorneys on Long Island, but being lawyered up came with a price tag.

Price's chest tightened as he swiveled around in his chair and gazed out the floor-to-ceiling window from his office's ninth-floor suite. He loved the lifestyle he had carved out for himself and Sable, and he wasn't ready to give it all up. Price could feel new bristles sprouting on his once freshly shaved dome. He was badly in need of a shape-up, but first things first. He retrieved his suit jacket from the closet, slipping it on over his crisp monogrammed dress shirt.

Selena escorted Waterburg into his office. The two men shook hands before Waterburg set his giant leather briefcase on the pale taupe carpet. Price reminded Selena to hold all calls before she returned to her desk, enveloping them in privacy.

Forty minutes later, the men emerged from their meeting with an ironclad strategy intact, guaranteeing Price's lifestyle and freedom. All he had to do was stick to the agreed-upon installment agreement that the IRS agents had set up.

Price returned to the window, fascinated by the golden fuchsia brush strokes that accented the August sky. With each subsequent breath, the tightness in his chest slowly faded.

Price made a quick call to his barber as he left the office for the day, thankful that the man's schedule meshed with his own. It was time to groom up. Chantel was waiting.

Juices's Jiggle Joint was popping that night. Price and his best friend, PJ, were seated right in front of Amethyst's gyrating treasure chest. She turned, revealing her perfectly sculpted back and taut buttocks, which ended in strong, well-cut, long legs. Her back flip revealed the pear-shaped jewel piercing, for which she was named, that winked between her legs.

"So, when are you gonna make me an uncle?" PJ asked.

"Soon, man. We're banging like bunnies."

"Maybe you should have Sable checked out."

"Already did. The doctor said she's fine."

Price's body drooled sweat as he squeezed in a round of Saturday afternoon golf during one of summer's dog days. A text from Chantel instantly threw his game into a freefall, and he hauled his overheated body into the golf cart.

Are you roasting?

I sure am. I am well done.

Ooh, I like my meat well done.

He ran three lights in his haste to get home. He showered and dressed, telling Sable just enough to get by. Online shopping and a bottle of merlot were his friends once again.

A condom-ready Price met Chantel for dinner at the Vault, a discreet little spot off Exit 33 of the Expressway, named not for its dining area but for the intimate ambiance of the suites situated directly behind it. The friendly blond restaurant greeter led them into a candlelit dining area, sitting them at a table for two.

The waiter came, and Price ordered for them both, quickly sending him on his way. A few minutes later, the waiter returned with a bottle of wine. He poured a glass for Price, and, upon Price's approval, a glass for Chantel as well. He reappeared with oysters on the half shell and steamed mussels before leaving the couple alone.

Leaving behind half-eaten appetizers and skipping the entrée entirely, Price and Chantel retired to their suite. He sank into a leather chair, inviting her to sit, too. With her back to him, she perched on his lap. His fingers found their way into the pastor's candy dish, getting them both hot and bothered. Then she stood and walked toward the bed.

He was about to follow, but she told him gently, "No, sit back and relax."

She tossed the comforter to the floor and eased back onto the sheets, rewarding him with a glimpse of her fresh Brazilian as she hiked up her dress. Price strained for more before she closed up shop.

Now, her fingers slid into the candy dish. "You want some?" she asked softly, cocking her head to the side.

His eyes never left hers. Price struggled to remain seated as she slid a finger into her mouth, satisfying her sweet tooth.

"You probably wouldn't even know what to do if I gave you some more," she toyed.

Price stood, unbuckled his belt, and unzipped his fly. He proved her wrong.

When Sable couldn't reach Price that night, she called David.

"Adonis knows about us," she told him. "We're in trouble."

"Are you sure?"

"Positive. He saw all of us that day in the city, leaving the Marriott."

David sighed. "He paid me a visit a few days later. Now it all makes sense. I'll handle Adonis."

Chapter 23

Thanks to his editor's email marked URGENT, Adonis was up at dawn, a second cup of coffee by his side. His fingers flew on the keyboard as he pounded out the last chapter of *Cheat Like a Lady, Snatch Like a Man*. If the manuscript's first draft was not in her inbox by the close of business, then the advance had better be repaid in full.

Adonis couldn't return money he didn't have. He wrapped up Bubbles' story and moved on to Sable, saving the best for last. What he didn't know, he made up.

Alejandra was soon blowing up Adonis's phone. "We need to talk," she told him.

He didn't like her tone. "About?"

"You'll find out when you get here," she said.

"Can it wait?"

"No."

Adonis checked his watch and decided to take a break from the manuscript. If he hurried, he'd have time to finish when he returned. Half an hour later, he was at her door.

"So, what's this all about?" he asked, seated in her living room.

"Maya, Nicholas, take Elliott and go play," she told her five-year-old.

"Okay, Mommy," Maya said, picking up Elliott.

Two-year-old Elliott struggled to be set free, flinging his legs to and fro. "No, no," he screamed.

"Put him down. He can walk," Alejandra said wearily, and they walked out of the room.

She started right in on him. "It's about your book. Why didn't you tell me Sable's in it?"

"I told you," he insisted.

"No, you didn't."

"I did."

"You told me about Tootsie and Bubbles."

"Sorry, my bad."

"Sable's off limits. Take her out of your rotation."

"Why?"

She had so many reasons why, but she settled for one big one. "Everyone wanted me to have an abortion, but because of Sable, I have Maya."

Adonis returned home and slammed the door behind him. He tweaked the last few chapters of *Cheat Like a Lady, Snatch Like a Man*. He'd screw Sable royally within the pages of his book as he referred to her and all the other women by first name only. And the sweetest part was that the names would remain the same, the spelling so thinly veiled that a kid could do the math. Only a phone call from Pastor Dante stopped him from hitting "send." His mind instantly flashed back to the stolen check and forward to the possibilities of more. "Send" could wait.

"Hello?" Adonis asked.

"Brother Watson, it's Pastor Dante."

"What can I do for you, Pastor Dante?"

"Brother Watson, I need you to come down to the church."

"Okay, I'll stop by this afternoon."

"No, not later. Now."

"What's this about?" Adonis asked.

"Your funeral," Pastor Dante said before hanging up.

Twenty minutes later, Adonis sat in the pastor's office. Adonis glanced around, waiting for the big surprise.

"There's something I want you to see," Pastor Dante began, turning his laptop toward Adonis.

Adonis gazed at the screen. There he was, plain as day, thumbing through Pastor Dante's Bible and pocketing the check. Pastor Dante turned off the computer and eased back into his chair.

"Brother Watson, I may be wearing a collar, but don't get it twisted. I will nail your ass to the cross." He picked up the phone and leaned forward. "I can call the cops right now, and we can get that orange jumpsuit ready, or I can use this clip as insurance against your sophomoric writing attempts and what you think you saw at the Marriott. Third strike, right?"

Adonis couldn't believe a church would take video of their own damn minister's office. "Okay, Rev, hang up."

"Smart decision," Pastor Dante agreed.

"So, off the record, what was that check for?"

Pastor Dante clasped his hands behind his neck and shook his head. "That's on a need-to-know."

"Damn, if that's how the big dogs roll, I'm in the wrong business."

"You have no idea."

"Then hit me with it."

"If I tell you," Pastor Dante said slowly, "I'd have to kill you."

Chapter 24

Tootsie was through being Mrs. Tootsie White-Storm. The future she envisioned as a child hadn't included a kinky husband who wanted his wife passed around like hot buttered popcorn. Life was cruel, hard, tough. She didn't need a magnifying glass to detect the cracks in her heart. Worse than that, she looked exactly like what she had been through—all three hundred self-medicated, hypertensive, gum-popping, acne-prone pounds of her.

She could explode at a moment's notice and consume everything in her path. Tootsie was tired of living by other folks' rules—first her mother's, then her husband's. All her life, Tootsie had abided by her mother's dictates. Never mind show business; Lilly was in the "no" business. From an early age, Tootsie learned that the answer to every question she asked her mother would be no, unless she had an exceptionally good reason to expect otherwise. No wonder she had clung to her virginity like a driver hugging the curves before plunging down an embankment. It was one of the few things left in her control. The more insulating pounds she packed on, the less male attention she garnered.

Tootsie blinked one morning, and she was nineteen. She blinked again, and she was thirty, then thirty-five. Though the years flew by with a vengeance, her luggage remained neatly packed under the bed because she was too timid to tip out the door. How many times had she pulled out her bag in a moment of frustrating rage, only to timidly slide it underneath a bed of submission? Yes, she was mad at the world, but mostly she was disgusted with herself. Life had no dress rehearsals, only this steady march of days that was swiftly passing her by.

One summer, two snakes. Adonis had sweet-talked her out of her most prized possession, only to gather material for a book. No doubt a special spot awaited him the day he busted hell wide open.

Wilson was another level of evil. Why had she gotten mixed up with this toenail-clipping, peanut-popping, dirty bird in the first place? What secret had Wilson dangled over Lilly White's precious head, which in turn caused her to push the promise of a modest diamond ring on her desperate daughter's itchy left ring finger? Only a scandalous mess could be threatening the manipulative missionary. What didn't she want leaked, and just how much dancing had Lilly done with this devil?

Tootsie checked the caller ID and rolled her eyes. *What does that woman want now?*

"Yes, Mama?" she answered. "What is it?" Whatever it was, she didn't have time for it.

"What is it?" Lilly repeated.

Tootsie held her ground and said nothing.

"We need to talk."

"About?"

"Just bring your butt over here."

"Look, Mama, I don't have time for—"

Lilly had already hung up.

"Shit," Tootsie said out loud. She rolled over and checked the clock on the nightstand. Now she'd have to cancel her one o'clock mani-pedi appointment. Tootsie scooted out of bed and jumped in the shower. That woman would be the death of her yet.

***

"So, what's so important, Mama, that it couldn't wait?" Tootsie joined her mother in the kitchen.

"Pull up a chair, daughter. Wait a minute. I just made a fresh pot of coffee. Pour Mama a cup."

"What would you do if I wasn't here, Mama?"

"That's why I got you, daughter."

Tootsie stood, shaking her head. She grabbed a mug from the dish rack and poured Lilly a cup. "Anything else while I'm up?"

"Grab me a bag of cookies from my cookie closet."

Tootsie opened the cabinet. "What kind?"

"Don't matter. Mama ain't picky."

"Good to know." Tootsie grabbed a pack of chocolate chip cookies before slamming her behind into a kitchen chair. "I'm missing a nail appointment. Talk to me."

"Wilson came to see me the other day. He's not pleased with you. Maybe you should put as much energy into your marriage as you do those acrylic nails of yours."

"Don't start, Mama. You don't know the half of it."

"I know one thing. If you wanna keep booking those appointments, you best take care of your husband."

"Look, Mama—"

"No, you look, daughter. Get your act together or else."

"Or else what?" Tootsie asked. "You don't know the humiliation that man has put me through. Don't thread my needle unless you've walked in my shoes."

"Me, me, me," Lilly repeated. "It's all about you."

"All about me? I only married Wilson because of you."

"Grow up, Tootsie. Be a woman."

"Like you, Mama? You can read all about me in *Cheat Like a Lady, Snatch Like a Man*. Are you in print yet, Mama?"

"Help me, Jesus." Lilly gasped as her head hit the cookies and her eyes rolled back in her head.

"Mama!" Tootsie jumped up and grabbed Lilly by the neck. "Wake up."

Lilly's lifeless body slumped back down onto the table. Tootsie felt for her pulse.

"Mama?" Tootsie grabbed the kitchen phone and called 9-1-1. "Hurry," she warned them.

Next, she called Bubbles. "Pick up, Bubbles. Pick up. Bubbles, I'm over my mother's. She's not breathing."

"Did you call an ambulance?"

"Of course I did."

"Does she have a pulse?"

"I think so."

"I'm coming over."

"Thanks, Bubbles," Tootsie told her before hanging up.

Tootsie ran to the living room and unlocked the front door before returning to her mother's side. An ambulance arrived a few minutes later.

"Back here." Tootsie motioned to them from the kitchen table.

Two EMT workers came in with a stretcher. By the time they reached the kitchen doorway, Lilly had come to.

"Ma'am, do you know what happened? How are you feeling?" the female EMT worker asked.

"I'm . . . I'm okay," she said, focusing on Tootsie.

"Can you tell us your name and address?" the male asked.

Lilly did as she was told.

They took her blood pressure and temperature before checking her pupils. "Any lightheadedness, chest pains, tingling, numbness?" the male technician asked.

Lilly shook her head. "No."

"Can you raise your arms for us?" the female worker asked.

Lilly raised both arms.

"Good," she told her.

"Let's check your tongue," he said.

Lilly stuck out her tongue.

"Good," he told her.

"Is this your mother?" the female EMT worker asked Tootsie.

"Yes."

"Were you here when she passed out?"

"Yes."

"What was she doing right before she passed out?"

"Having a snack—coffee and cookies."

"That's a lot of sugar."

"Well, Missionary White, your vitals are normal, but would you like to go to the hospital for observation?" the female technician asked.

"No, I'm fine."

"Can you walk for us?" the male asked.

"Can I walk? I'm not crippled," she shot back.

"Let's see," the female EMT worker said gently.

"Hmmph, this don't make no kinda sense."

With their assistance, she rose to her feet and walked to the sink and back.

"Okay, you seem to be fine."

The female EMT worker completed a report while the younger technician collapsed the stretcher.

"Call back if you change your mind," he reminded Lilly and Tootsie.

"We will," Tootsie agreed as she saw them out.

Bubbles arrived just as the ambulance left.

"Missionary White, are you feeling okay?" Bubbles asked.

"Of course I'm okay. Why wouldn't I be?" Lilly told her.

"Mama, she was worried about you."

"Take your slutty behind and your slutty buddy and get out of my house. Now," Lilly yelled.

"This isn't over, Mama," Tootsie warned her. She headed to the door, then turned to her friend.

"Come on, Bubbles. Let's get outta here."

"I'm starving. Wanna get something to eat?"

"Sure." Tootsie pulled her car keys from her purse. "I'll drive."

Within minutes, she was on the Conduit headed toward Green Acres Mall. Half an hour later, they were seated at a booth in Red Lobster.

"So, what's up with your mother?" Bubbles frowned. "I know I'm not her fave person, but damn."

Tootsie stirred her mudslide. "Girl, she's just pulling you into my mess. Don't pay her no mind."

"What happened?"

"Adonis is what happened. He's writing this book about the last twelve women he's slept with called *Cheat Like a Lady, Snatch Like a Man*. I tried to warn Mama and she flipped out, playing her holier-than-thou card—again."

"Oh." Bubbles sipped her martini slowly.

"Oh? Is that all you have to say? You know something, Bubbles? I tell you all of my business, while you share none of yours."

"What do you want me to say?"

"Say how you feel."

"Okay. I'm scared."

"Why scared?" Tootsie asked.

"Because I slept with Adonis too."

Tootsie sat at the kitchen table in her bathrobe, smoking a cigarette and nursing her second glass of wine. With each sip, she played the leave-him, leave-him-not game until she drained the goblet.

As if on cue, Wilson appeared in the doorway and headed to the counter to pour himself a drink. Tootsie stiffened in the wooden chair as he turned toward her. She refused to meet his gaze, concentrating instead on her chipped red nail polish.

"Why aren't you dressed?" Wilson asked his bride. "Don't have me waiting all night."

She drummed her fingers on the tabletop as she tried to find the right words. Then the way out hit her. *Hell, just say it.*

She looked him dead in the eye. "This ain't working for me."

"So, you were a little nervous the first time. That's why I gave you a pass. Let's try again tonight. Get dressed."

"No, I'm not going." She tightened the bathrobe around her robust middle.

"What did you say?" He removed his glasses as if he'd hear better.

"Put your damn glasses back on, Wilson. You heard me. I'm not going."

"But you said—"

"Don't tell me what I said. I know what I said. I changed my mind."

"You listen to me." His voice grew low and steady.

"No, let's flip that. I don't care if you drop your voice till it hits the floor. I'm not going."

"I'm giving you the chance to bed any man you want. Check your mirror, honey. Men ain't lining up to get with you. You should be grateful for this opportunity."

"Whatever," she told him.

"Look, are you in or are you out?"

"I told you. I'm out." She reached for her wine.

"You can change your mind all you want, but if I walk out this door, you can forget about me coming back for you," he warned.

"Already forgotten."

"Don't wait up."

"Hmmph, I never do."

"You know something? You ought to bow down on your hands and knees and suck my big toe for marrying your ass."

She pruned up her face at the nauseating visual. "You disgust me."

A low, guttural sound reverberated from Wilson's throat. "On second thought, you look exhausted. Stay in and relax. Read any good books lately?" He reached inside his pocket and threw a copy in her direction.

It landed in her lap, and she read the title. "Who the hell is Madam Magnolia?"

A showdown-ready Tootsie picked her mother's front door lock with a stolen dental scaler. She stormed into her mother's bedroom, pushing the door open with such force that the hangers behind it toppled to the floor along with the clothes on them. Missionary White jumped, spilling red nail polish all over her sheets.

"Is it true?" Tootsie screamed.

"Look what you made me do." Lilly reached for the box of tissues on her nightstand to wipe up the mess. Smearing it, of course, only made matters worse. "Better get some bleach." Lilly stripped the bed and headed for the bathroom.

Still breathing hard from running up the stairs, Tootsie wasn't going to be distracted. "Is it true?"

"Is what true, daughter?"

Tootsie blocked the doorway, making it impossible for Lilly to pass. "Don't you dare walk away from me."

Lilly grunted and returned to the bed, shaking her head. "This don't make no kinda sense. I don't know what's gotten into you."

"Really, Lilly? Or should I say Priscilla Lee?"

The name caused her mother to drop her mouth open. "I don't know what Wilson told you, but it's not—"

"That's all I needed to hear." Tootsie turned to leave.

"Tootsie, wait." Lilly jumped in front of her.

"Get out of my way."

"Let me explain."

"Oh, now you wanna talk? Move out my way."

"Tootsie, judge not lest ye be judged also."

"You think those ankle-skimming, down-to-the-ground dresses will save you?"

"Jesus. The blood of Jesus," Lilly pleaded.

Tootsie got all up in her face. "You look down your nose at me for getting my cherry popped at thirty-five when you—"

"Tootsie, please." Lilly covered her ears.

"But at least I wasn't selling it wholesale. Or was that retail, Mama?"

"Enough," Lilly yelled.

"No, it's not enough. You sold me to the highest bidder."

"That's not true, daughter. I swear to God that's not true." Lilly's head shook in spasms.

"Payback's a mother, just like you. I plan on writing a book about you. It'll make Adonis's book look like 'Jack and Jill.'"

"Tootsie, no."

"Get away from me."

"Listen to me." Lilly grabbed Tootsie's throat, squeezing hard.

Tootsie's breath got caught in her windpipe. When she recovered from her surprise, she elbowed her mother, hard, and she fell to the floor.

"I'm leaving." She stepped over Lilly like day-old trash.

"Tootsie, wait. Please don't go." She clung to her daughter's shoe.

Tootsie shook her foot free. "We're done."

She stormed out of her mother's bedroom, deaf to the sobs and pleas for forgiveness. She went straight to her own bedroom and flipped on the light switch. Everything seemed untouched, just as she had left it before her wedding. She got down on her hands and knees and pulled the dust bunny–covered suitcase from underneath her bed. Sneezing, she wiped it off with the bed skirt before reaching for a tissue from the nightstand to blow her nose.

She took one last look around the room—the faded green wallpaper, the chipped paint on the ceiling, the worn bedspread and matching curtains, and she realized: She would never return.

Tootsie finished up breakfast. With each sip of coffee, she wrestled with her herself—to write the book about her mother, or not write the book. She deliberately took small sips, savoring the deep-roasted flavor of the Colombian brew. The last sip clinched it. No book.

Tootsie called her mother later that night. "Mama, I just want you to know that I thought it over. I won't be writing that book after all. Nope."

"Thank God, you've come to your senses. Your mama ain't raised no fool."

Tootsie didn't miss the relief in her voice. Nope.

Chapter 25

"Just when I thought you couldn't look any more radiant," Price said, gazing at Chantel. As if on cue, a server came by and took their orders.

Three hours and four drinks later, he reached for her hand and pulled her up. "Let's get outta here."

Price unlocked the door to a private room and closed the door behind them. Chantel wrapped her arms around his neck as she kissed him back.

"Turn around." He bent her over the arm of the loveseat before plunging into her wetness. Price grabbed her by the ponytail and went deep as he stood tall. Then, with their knees propped up on the loveseat, he massaged her shoulders and slowly kissed the back of her neck. With one hand, he fondled her, while the other hand slid between her thighs.

Chantel could no longer hold back. The moans that had been percolating in her throat finally escaped, bringing her to an insane climax. Drenched in sweat, Price lapped up the liquid gold dripping from his fingers before flipping her over onto her back.

"I'm licking up all that honey between your thighs tonight." He snapped her knees open and dived in, forcing Chantel to cum again and again.

Catching her breath, she pulled him up by the ear and deeply kissed him on the mouth. Their tongues savor the sweetest caress as she opened her thighs and his erection hit home.

***

Too drunk to pop in his contacts, Price whistled through his Monday until a FedEx delivery wiped the smile right off his face. He ripped open the envelope, unable to miss the IRS return address. He extracted the notice's contents, and his eyes nearly popped out of their sockets when he read and reread the bottom line. Preoccupied with life, he had missed two payments. *FINAL NOTICE.* His time was up. Where was he going to get over half a million dollars? He reached for the fifth of vodka that he kept in the lower right-hand drawer of his desk. The first swig of the day was always the best, quenching his thirst with that loving burn his body always craved. By the third gulp, the bottle was half empty. He reached for its twin stashed in the lower left-hand drawer and polished that off, too.

Price pulled keys from his pocket and stopped. What were Sable's car keys doing in his pocket? Then the light came on: he was driving Midnight these days. Keeping it dignified, he adjusted his jacket and tie before staggering out the door.

Half an hour later, Price was propped up at Juice's Jiggle Joint, guzzling down his second blackberry martini. Juices's bartenders kept the drinks long and strong. Price had no complaints. Cocktails mixed with the naked girls' hypnotic gyrations propelled Price's brain into another dimension, and he guzzled down two more. He squinted at the smoke-filled bar while strippers worked a pair of poles. Were there three girls on stage or four? Switching to shots furthered the odyssey, upping his sense of omnipotence until he almost shut down the Joint.

He threw a few bills on the bar, nodded at the bartender, and headed for the door. A chipped tooth caught his attention on the way out. Price could swear that the checkerboard thug was entering just as he was exiting.

Adonis shook his head as he entered Juice's and headed toward the bar. *I cashed your check, arrogant bastard.* Price was ripped, but hell, Adonis needed to get his swerve on like anybody else.

Adonis ordered a whiskey sour, double-checking the tiny wad in his pocket to make sure he could pay for it first. He couldn't believe he had gone through all the money from Pastor Dante's check and the book advance on back rent and living expenses. Now what the hell was he to do? They could put a man on the moon. You'd think they'd find a way to attach an ATM to a pussy.

He hated saying goodbye to *Cheat Like a Lady, Snatch Like a Man.* It was probably the great American novel— or at least one of those Lifetime movies—but any day not spent behind bars was a good one.

Adonis ordered another drink, his ball getting hard as he watched the girls weave their web of wickedness. He grabbed his crotch, longing for a lap dance. Gone were the days when he could make it rain.

Adonis lit a cigarette, nursing his drink with one hand while smoking with the other. The stool next to him became vacant, then occupied just as quickly. Deep in thought, Adonis ignored the transition. Only when the man ordered a drink did the raspy voice register with Adonis. He knew instantly. It was Tootsie's husband.

"What's going on?" Wilson asked.

"Whassup, man?" Adonis gave him the up-nod.

"She did us both foul," Wilson grunted.

Adonis bit his tongue, choosing instead to take another puff from his Marlboro. He let Wilson continue.

"Bitch left me. Whore just like her mama. A missionary-fronting slut. Calls herself Lilly White these days. Trust me, she ain't. Brags about spending a lot of time on her knees."

"Like strippers and hoes." Adonis raised his glass in a toast because the wheels in his mind were already beginning to spin.

"You looking for a slippery cast of characters? Church never fails." Wilson winked. "That's the place to be. The game remains the same, only the players change."

A ho turned missionary. Adonis sucked down the last of his whiskey, paid his tab, and jetted out the door. His editor was waiting.

Chapter 26

Damn straight she wouldn't be writing that book. It would take too long. Tootsie had another plan, a better plan.

Early Sunday morning, she entered the church with a giant weekender bag. The dimly lit sanctuary was empty. Tootsie wheeled the bag down the purple runner of the center aisle and stopped at the front pew. Then she turned and walked a bit farther to the pulpit and choir stand.

Tootsie eased herself down and unzipped the bag, reaching inside for a stack of the special programs she had made at Staples. With a hand on her knee, she took a deep breath and struggled back upright. She placed a three-page program on the pulpit and several on each pew from the choir stand to the door. She finished just as the first church members filed in. Priscilla Lee's story was now in place.

Tootsie took a seat in the far corner of the last pew. She watched the church fill up. A rushing wind from the open doors caused the papers on the pews to rustle, swirling around their heads. Members reached up and snatched the program in midair, eager to read the scarlet inserts.

Tootsie saw the hallelujah-hat meander down the center catwalk until Lilly plopped down in her usual fourth-row pew. What started out as a few scattered whispers escalated to loud, animated chatter as the electrifying pulse of the congregation's shock and disbelief swept the sanctuary.

First came that familiar gasp, then the hallelujah hat hit the floor, followed by a frantic call for an ambulance. Lilly was circling the drain, and Tootsie was all churched out. She headed for the exit as her mother's past went live.

Her lips curled up in a smile as she lugged the weekender down the steps. She had endured enough madness to last three lifetimes. It was time to move on. Maybe she always had the power to click her heels, not to go home again like Dorothy, but to finally leave home. She wiped away a tear, cutting the cord and kissing her old life goodbye.

With a cab waiting at the curb, Tootsie left her season of anger behind. Mission—or rather missionary—accomplished.

Chapter 27

Returning home from a late business meeting, Price joined Sable in the kitchen.

"I'm knocked out," he announced, grabbing a chair to sit.

She greeted him from behind, massaging his neck and shoulders. "Feel like some coffee, babe?"

"Okay."

Sable grabbed their favorite mugs from the cabinet and popped a K-Cup in the Keurig. She filled both mugs with coffee, making sure his was just the way he liked it before she sat down.

Price reached across the table, taking both of her hands in his. He needed her now more than ever. He searched Sable's eyes, drawing upon her warmth, gentleness, and patience for strength. Her unconditional love and acceptance gave him the courage to reveal the truth.

He tried swallowing the lump in his throat before another one appeared. Price took a deep breath. "First of all, I need you to swear to me that you will not repeat a word of what I'm about to tell you."

"Of course, babe," she agreed.

"Okay." He rubbed his face, which was badly in need of a shave, and took a sip of coffee. "A couple of weeks ago, I was having a couple of drinks at the bar with PJ. Anyway, I'd had a few too many, and I bumped into Adonis on the way out."

"Okay."

"He needn't breathe the same air as me. Bad attitude. I could've killed him with my bare hands, but I took the high road and walked out the door. I hopped in Midnight and drove off, but all I could see was that smirk on his face. I got on the Southern State and nearly collided with a car weaving in and out of traffic. It's crazy, but we started drag racing. Then I got a text. I took my eye off the road for a second to check my phone, and he was gone.

"I slowed down until visions of Adonis popped up, and I just lost it. I wanted to snap his windpipe. I flew down the highway and nearly missed the exit. Out of nowhere, this figure appeared in front of the car, but I couldn't stop in time."

Sable jumped up, leaning against the island for support. Her hand flew to her mouth as her eyes grew large as dessert plates.

"Turned out to be a bear."

"Thank you, Jesus."

Even in the air-conditioned kitchen, the thin robe clung wetly to Price's back and armpits as he relived the nightmare. "When I woke up the next morning, a story about an accident on the Southern State was all over the news. The drag-racing car was totally mangled, the driver and a man walking alongside the road were both killed. So, if I hadn't slowed down to check my phone . . ."

"Oh my God!"

"Exactly."

Sable shut her eyes before covering them with her hand.

"Maybe if we hadn't been racing, he would have had enough time to slow down and avoid hitting him."

She returned to the table and sat in his lap, gently wiping away his tear. "Look at me, honey. You don't know that for sure. Don't take on that guilt. You didn't kill anyone. That other driver did. He was already driving erratically, weaving in and out of traffic. He probably couldn't have stopped even if he wanted to. They said his blood alcohol level was double the legal limit."

"I hate to think what mine was," Price said.

"Me too," she admitted. "That text was a blessing in disguise. It prevented death from coming in threes."

"God saved me that night," he said softly. "He's real."

"Yes, he is, Price. Sometimes God brings you right to the edge and lets you peek over that cliff before he snatches you back. He has a way of making us stop, look, and listen to Him."

Sable soaked in each new day and night with her husband. She was thankful for second chances and restored love. She and Price rocked a honeymoon glow.

"You're right. Be patient with me, baby. I just need some time to process all this, ya know?"

"You've changed," Sable said slowly as she looked into his eyes and rubbed the back of his head. "And I like it. It's a good thing."

"It's a God thing." He took her in his arms for a long embrace.

Finally, she came up for air. "Honey, are you sure you don't want to go out for your birthday? I can still make reservations."

"No, babe, a quiet evening at home with you is all I need."

"Okay, let me slip into something more—"

The peal of the doorbell cut her short.

"That's Tito's Rib Shack. I'll make a nice home-cooked meal tomorrow night, I promise," she told him.

Price left to answer the door. Sable reached for her purse when her phone rang.

"Can you talk?" It was Alejandra.

"Everything okay?" Sable asked.

"It's wonderful. I won't keep you, but I got the job at the hospital. I start next week. Childcare on the premises, health insurance, dental . . . Your navy-blue suit nailed it."

"No, your navy-blue suit nailed it. I'm so happy for you."

"I can't thank you enough, Sable."

"You just did," she insisted.

Sable climbed the stairs as Price paid the delivery boy. He peeked inside the shopping bag, allowing the familiar aromas to escape while he made his way to the kitchen. When he returned to the great room, Sable was already seated, legs crossed, dangling a stiletto off her foot. Her arm was extended along the top of the sofa.

"Baby, this is the best birthday ever."

"Even without cake?"

"You're my cake, baby."

"Mmm, I like that. Wanna go play in my frosting?" she whispered in his ear, grinning seductively.

Price stood and pulled Sable to her feet, then scooped her up in his arms. That night, they made love like the time they first met—hot, juicy, passionate, wet. He creamed Sable's cupcake, and she couldn't wait to blow out Price's candle, checking his last box.

After Midnight came La Dawn. Price gassed up his wife's new ride and made sure all was well. La Dawn wasn't a Benz, but driving American was the new fabulous and within their means. Sable was all smiles as the darkness of midnight became a part of their past and they made way for a bright future.

They arrived at the office building where they'd been summoned to a meeting, along with Chantel and David. They went inside, and a tall, curly-haired man approached

them. His periwinkle tie provided the perfect pop of color
for his navy pinstripe suit and crisp white shirt.

"Pastor and First Lady Dante, Mr. and Mrs. Galore,
I'm Kevin Clayton, Gus De Angelo's attorney. Let's talk
inside." He motioned for them to accompany him.

They took a seat in his office before he closed the door.
"Thanks for coming."

"We're not sure why we're here," David admitted.

Mr. Clayton nodded. "You'll see." He slid a disc into
the DVD player and then grabbed the gunmetal-colored
remote to start the TV.

The screen was black until bold white letters appeared
along with a soundtrack of The Hollies' "He Ain't Heavy . . .
He's My Brother.":

> Sister Galore, I was thirsty, and you gave me
> water. I was hungry, and you fed me. When you do
> for the least of your brethren, you do it for me. Pastor
> Dante, holiness churches preach that you have to
> speak in tongues to be saved. As a mute, I could
> never speak in tongues. You made me see that so
> long as I spoke with my heart I, too, could be saved.
> Mucho dinero en amor.

Sable shook her head. The video didn't make sense.
Then she saw the scar as his face leaped onto the screen.
Gus De Angelo was the homeless man she had befriended.

> All most people see is my scar. Thank you both for
> looking beyond it and seeing me.

Mr. Clayton stopped the tape. "Mr. De Angelo was
killed in that car accident a couple of days ago. It was all
over the news."

"Oh, no, not Gus," Sable said as Price put his arm around her and squeezed her shoulder.

"He was such a kind man," Chantel said.

"Our condolences to his family," David added.

"Mrs. Galore, Gus left you $950,126."

"What?" Sable's eyes widened. She pressed her hand against her chest, her fingers spread out. "Wait a minute. Is this for real?"

"It certainly is, Mrs. Galore."

Sable shook her head slowly, and unbidden tears raced down her cheeks. She wiped them away. "Unbelievable."

Mr. Clayton slid the glasses up his nose. "Pastor Dante, your church shall inherit five hundred thousand dollars, provided that this gift remains anonymous, too."

"Too?" David asked.

"Yes, Gus anonymously donated fifty thousand dollars to the One Way Church earlier this summer."

"That was Gus?" he asked.

Mr. Clayton nodded.

Pastor Dante sucked in a quick breath and clasped his fingers behind his neck. "So now I know."

Chapter 28

The Dantes and the Galores went to Miami Beach for a long weekend. They unpacked and settled into their suites for the night. Sable stretched and rolled over as her husband slept soundly by her side.

His eyes flickered open, and he smiled. "Morning, beautiful."

"Morning." She cuddled up next to him.

By late afternoon, they were all ready for a nap. They barely made it to their rooms, crashing in the living room and dozing off.

Sable got up and headed to the bathroom before she finally returned to the sofa. Knocked out, they ordered in and called it a night.

Sable slept in the next morning. Awakened by laughter coming from the living room, she got up and joined the others.

"Hey, sleepy head," Chantel greeted her.

"Girl, I was knocked out." Sable yawned as she reached for her purse on the table.

"Must be all this island sun," Chantel told her.

"And the extra strength vitamin D," David added.

They broke out in laughter until a pregnancy test fell from Sable's purse, shutting it down. Price bent down and picked up the test before he tossed it onto the table.

"I'm sorry," Sable said simply.

"Whose is it?" David asked.

"It's yours," Price responded.

"How can you be so sure?" Chantel asked.

"I'm sterile," Price admitted.

"Are you sure?" Chantel asked.

"I'm positive."

"Hold up. Wait, babe. Sterile?" Sable frowned. "What are you talking about?"

"You know I went to college on a full football scholarship, and that my sports career ended in my junior year with a groin injury."

"Uh-huh."

"What I never told anyone is that that injury left me sterile."

The two embraced.

"But why didn't you tell me?"

"When we first met, I assumed that, like most women, you wanted to be a mother, but when I realized that that wasn't your priority, I didn't feel the need to discuss."

"So, what are we going to do?" David asked, his eyes searching Sable's.

Sable shrugged. "Looks like we're all having a baby."

Just when Bubbles thought the four of them couldn't get any more tight-knit, she spotted a very pregnant Sable, along with First Lady and their husbands, entering Babies R Us. With her trusted binoculars by her side, Bubbles waited. As they exited with two shopping carts full of baby merchandise, Bubbles got out of her car and into a heated confrontation with Price.

"No, you're the fool," she told him. "You up here buying out the store when you don't even know if the baby is yours."

"Honey, that ain't none of your business," Sable shot back.

"Well, when he finds out that it ain't—"

"Oh, you must think this baby is gonna break us up and my husband will suddenly choose you." Sable laughed, and the others joined in. "Babe, how dumb is that? Doesn't she realize that this baby is a symbol of our love? Let's load up the cars and get out of here. I need my rest."

Bubbles stepped up her stalking of the couples, even going so far as to park across the street from Sable's house to monitor their home. Apparently, Sable complained to Price, who had a run-in with Bubbles across the street.

"What's your problem?" he said. "I told you a long time ago, stay away from my family. Stay away from my house. Don't make me call the cops."

"Darling, I'm just enjoying the breeze. That's all. You're being paranoid."

Price tried a different approach. "What do you want, Bubbles? Huh? What do you really want?"

"I want you," she said simply

"That's impossible. Not happening. I moved on."

"Then get ready to be destroyed. You and your household will all be destroyed."

"Is that a threat?"

"It's a promise. Keep screwing around and find out." She started up the engine and drove off.

Later that night, Bubbles camped out in the hotel parking lot and checked her phone. Again. *Damn, they're emptying the clip tonight,* she said under her breath. She folded her arms and waited for their return.

The two couples exited well after midnight, looking totally relaxed. Laughing and smiling, they walked toward their cars. Bubbles pulled up next to them and rolled down her window. She spat on the ground next to David before looking him up and down.

"And you call yourself a pastor. You think you're getting away with it. You're not. Everybody's gonna get got. Keep rollin' around in the mud. You'll see. Mark my words. You'll all pay." She rolled up her window and drove off.

Chapter 29

Six months later, Baby Galore was born, screaming at the top of his lungs. Price cut the umbilical cord, and the nurse laid him on his mother's heart. Ten fingers. Ten toes. Sable was immediately in awe of the wide-eyed bundle. After giving thanks, Price got in bed and shared an intimate embrace with the love of his life and their new son before heading to the waiting area to share the good news with the Dantes.

"It's a boy!" Price beamed as David and Chantel stood. "Seven-and-a-half pounds, nineteen inches long. Healthy as can be."

"Aw, man." David pulled Price into a tight embrace. He wiped away tears for the son he could never claim. "How's Sable?"

"Sable is amazing and resting comfortably. We couldn't have hand-picked a better mother for our son. We've decided to name him Solomon. Solomon Dante Galore."

"Thanks, man." David's pain melted into gratitude.

Chantel was ecstatic. "Ooh, I can't wait to be a godmother."

Price grinned. "And he's going to love you as much as I do."

Sable and Price settle into their new life, their home fully baby-proofed and complete with a monitoring system, compliments of David and Chantel. Solomon had his first-time parents up at the crack of dawn, his wailing more predictable than the alarm on any clock.

Just over a month old, baby Solomon kept his mother busy. Sable got up for the third time that night, awakened by his fretful cries. She slid into her house slippers and headed into his room. She bent and scooped him up out of the crib and held him close. Touching his forehead and then rubbing his back, she whispered gently in his ear.

"It's okay. Mommy's here. It's okay."

His tiny heart was racing, and he was burning up. She sat and quickly took his temperature as Price now stood in the doorway.

"We need to get him to the emergency room."

The NICU team whisked baby Solomon away, his heart-wrenching cries echoing all the way down the hall and bringing Sable to tears. She and Price completed forms and paperwork as David and Chantel rushed to their sides.

"Thank God you're here," Sable said as a nurse returned their ID and insurance card. The four huddled together in corporate prayer led by David. They embraced afterward.

"We got here as quickly as we could," David told them.

"So, what happened?" Chantel asked gently.

Sable pieced together the events of the last week, including Solomon's routine doctor's appointment just days earlier, and culminating in the fever that brought them to the ER.

"Have the doctors told you anything?" David asked.

"Just that they'll be taking blood, running tests, and treating him to normalize his breathing and get the fever down," Sable said.

Just then, a doctor appeared, and the four stood, hopeful for good news. "Mr. and Mrs. Galore, I'm Dr. Malone. Can I speak to you in private?"

"It's okay," Price assured him. "This is our pastor and first lady, Solomon's godparents."

"I just wanted to update you on your son's condition. The first twenty-four hours are critical. It's too early to tell, but we're doing everything we can to keep him comfortable."

"Thank you," Price said, disappointed.

"We'll keep you posted regarding any changes. Try to get some rest," Dr. Malone advised before being paged and walking away.

"Looks like it's gonna be a long night. So, if you guys want to go home and get some rest . . ." Price suggested as they sat.

"Uh-uh. We wouldn't dream of leaving you guys at a time like this. We're staying right here. We're family, and we'll get through this together," Chantel assured him.

"I can't imagine life without baby Solomon," Sable admitted, searching her purse for tissue and blowing her nose.

"Com'ere," Price said gently. "It's going to be okay." He rubbed her shoulder.

They dozed off in their husband's arms. Early the next morning, Doctor Malone returned. He removed his glasses, his eyes bloodshot.

"We've given your son medication to reduce the fever, and his vitals are returning to normal quite nicely. I've never seen anyone in such distress respond so quickly. He's a miracle baby. We want to keep him another day for observation. If all goes well, we'll discharge him."

"Thanks, doctor," Sable and Price said in unison.

"Bless you," David added.

"Can we see him?" Sable brightened.

"And pray with him?" David added.

"Of course. And by the way," he added, "your son is a real trooper."

"Yes, he is," Price beamed as they headed in to see Solomon.

After another night of Hayden's hell, Bubbles woke up alone five hours later in the emergency room, hooked up to an IV machine. A female resident came in to check her condition. The blond doctor peered intently into Bubbles' eyes. Gently, she asked Bubbles about the lacerations and wounds that covered her body.

"What happened?" Dr. Fatner asked.

Bubbles looked away, afraid to blow her husband's cover. He had warned her: *Tonight stays between you and me. Understand?*

"I fell."

"Mrs. Legree, forgive me, but we have counselors and social workers on staff. We're here to help. Everything will be kept in strictest confidence. You're safe now. What happened to you is not your fault."

Bubbles smiled as best she could. "I know, doctor, but I fell."

"You fell," the doctor repeated.

"Yes." Bubbles struggled to keep her raccoon eyes open. "I fell."

"Okay, Mrs. Legree, but if you change your mind . . ."

"I fell."

"Okay, I'll be back a little later to check on you. We're going to admit you." She handed Bubbles a business card. "You may need this one day. Face to Face offers free plastic surgery for victims of domestic abuse."

"Thank you, doctor."

***

"Look who's awake," Sable boasted as the Dantes joined the Galores for brunch.

"How's our little man?" David asked, rubbing his head. "You gave us quite a scare."

"Yes, he did," Chantel agreed as the men headed to the den. "Can I help with anything?" she asked Sable.

"Let's see." Sable put her hands on her hips and looked around: salmon cakes, turkey bacon, pancakes, avocado, fruit, green tea, coffee. "Everything's almost ready. Ooh, Chantel, would you get the pitcher of fresh-squeezed juice and see if the biscuits are done?"

"Sure," Chantel said. "Sit and rest your feet. You've probably been on 'em all morning."

"Girl, I'm fine. I need to keep moving. I still have baby weight to lose. Don't act like you don't see it." She laughed.

"You're beautiful," Chantel said. "You always were, and you always will be."

"Aw, thanks."

"I swear Solomon's gone up another size since the last time we saw him. Right, honey?" Chantel said as the men returned.

"Ooh, it smells good up in here," Price said, checking out the table and ready to feast.

"That's some spread," David agreed before putting Solomon in his bassinet.

"Man, my wife has turned into Betty Crocker since the baby was born. It's like we went from take-out five nights a week to home-cooked meals every night. Got a brother loosening his belt," he told him as they all sat.

"This is the first time I've really been able to enjoy a meal since Solomon got sick," Sable admitted before Price said grace.

"But look at him now." David smiled. "Not a care in the world." As if on cue, Solomon squealed with delight, kicking his legs in agreement.

"God is so good." Chantel grinned.

"Truly," Sable said. "Dig in."

Awakened in the middle of the night by the sound of his ringing phone, David turned toward the nightstand and fumbled to retrieve it in the dark.

It was Bubbles. "Pastor Dante, I just wanted you to know that I'm in the hospital. Hayden beat me up bad. The doctors said my internal injuries were so severe, they're surprised that I pulled through. I had him arrested for domestic violence. I couldn't take it anymore. I couldn't take it anymore," she kept repeating.

"Which hospital?" he asked.

"Island General. They plan on keeping me a few more days."

"Are you up for visitors?" he asked.

"Not really," she admitted. "But please keep me in your prayers."

"Will do."

By now, Chantel was awake too. She leaned into her husband and placed her head on his chest. "We're here for you, Sister Bubbles. Let us know what we can do to help."

"Thank you," she said simply. "Oh, and Pastor, I'm sorry for all the hell I put you guys through when it was never my business to begin with. My eyes should have been watching God, but the whole time, I was really watching and listening to you guys."

"Hold on." He hit RECORD. "What do you mean?"

"Well, I hacked into all your phones, your group chats, and installed special software and cameras on all your devices that allowed me to view you in real time and record your keystrokes. I even put a tracking device on your cars. That's how I knew your every move."

"Wow," David exclaimed, mind blown.

"And tell First Lady that I was the one who created a fake social media account in her name and DM'd fake photos to Price. It was all me."

David and Chantel looked at each other in disbelief. It made no sense.

"So . . . I plan on taking a break from church to do some much-needed soul searching. I may even get re-baptized. I know I'm asking a lot, but I hope that one day the four of you can find it in your heart to forgive me."

David looked at Chantel before speaking. "You know, Sister Bubbles, it takes a special kind of person to admit when they've done wrong and humble themselves the way you just did."

"Thank you, Pastor. Please keep me in your prayers."

"Oh, I will," he said before hanging up. "God bless you."

"Oh my God." Chantel shook her head. "I remember feeling paranoid, like I was being watched, and all the while it was her. She stalked us and gaslit me to think that I was the one going crazy, when all the time we were being monitored. That's creepy. How did she find the time to do all that and endure Hayden's abuse too?"

"Can't make this stuff up," he insisted. "Know something? Maybe it's time we decide if our secret covenant is worth sacrificing our personal covenant with God."

"You're right. Let's meet to discuss."

David knew that asking permission was easier than begging forgiveness, but on some issues, God would never cosign. David knew better, and yet he was drowning in a tsunami of guilt that he had brought on himself.

Not only had he allowed Sable to seduce his body, but his integrity, too. He couldn't get enough of her. Yet, with each illicit romp, he risked plunging his ministry into gossipy tabloid fodder for the world to devour. Was it fair to blame Chantel for his fall from grace, or was she the scapegoat? Who was the man behind the pulpit? Like Jacob, he was a trickster, a deceiver. How could he preach another message or take communion again, let alone serve it?

The four met up at a quaint coffeehouse tucked away a few blocks from the mall. Coupled off, they spoke freely before getting back together for a final group discussion.

For a moment, neither Sable nor David spoke. She stirred her coffee in silence while he took a few sips of his.

"I can't do this anymore, David. I can't listen to you preach on Sunday mornings and then open my legs for you at night and call myself a woman of God. Some boxes are best left unchecked. I will always love you as the father of my child, but I keep hearing Bubbles' warning that we will pay. Look at Solomon. Thank God he's okay, but next time, God may not show us mercy. I can't afford to sacrifice our son on the altar of our lust. And my husband deserves a wife who only has eyes for him."

"Sable," David began. "As much as I adore you, this secret has been eating away at my soul, and pretty soon, there won't be anything left. Giving my son up was the hardest thing I've ever done. As a pastor, my punishment is never knowing if my passion for God is deeper than my passion for you, and I can't go on living in purgatory. My prayer is: Father forgive us, for we knew what we were doing, and we did it anyway."

They stood and shared a long embrace.

"Thank you," he whispered in her ear.

"For what?" Sable asked.

"For reconnecting me with my first love," he confessed.

"You're very welcome."

"Chantel, I can't lie. I had the Super Bowl of wives, and then you came along—sexy AF—and I had to have you too. We were both so selfish that we couldn't even play by the rules we made. All those private hook-ups? Hell yeah, they were fun, but even I know that God was not pleased. Chantel, we thought we had the best of both worlds, but we didn't. I can't do it anymore."

"Listen, Price," Chante told him. "I just want to hear Him say well done. Deep down inside, we know we're making a mockery of God. He's not cosigning on this nonsense, and I don't like what I see when I look in the mirror."

Price and Chantel joined their spouses.

"Looks like Bubbles won after all." Chantel shrugged. "We broke up, and that's all she wanted.

"Nobody wins. God always gets the last laugh," David said simply. "But my mother used to say that old lovers make the best friends. Let's prove her right."

"This is for you." Price placed a small, wrapped box in Sable's lap before they headed out to church with Solomon for his christening.

"For me?" she asked, removing the red satin bow and red wrapping paper. "This paper is so beautiful, I almost don't want to tear it."

"It's me, remember? Go ahead."

Sable opened the box and took a deep breath. Inside the black velvet-cushioned box sat a ruby baguette wedding band. "Oh, honey, it's perfect."

"Do you like it?"

"I love it. Here, put it on me." She switched the diamond to her right hand and held out her left ring finger.

"Read the inscription," he told her.

She read out loud, "Proverbs 31:10. Who can find a virtuous woman? Sable, I've found mine. Forever, Price."

Sable began to cry. "Babe . . ."

He kissed her tears away as he slid the new wedding band on her finger. "I know our big anniversary isn't until next year, but I couldn't wait. With you in my life, they're all big. Sable, you check all my boxes, and I'll do whatever it takes to check all of yours."

They embraced once more.

"Here's your gift," she said.

"Uh-uh, you're my gift. Remember?" He kissed her full lips. Price unsealed the envelope and read the card. "It's beautiful."

As he leaned forward to display the card on the coffee table, a smaller envelope landed at his feet. Puzzled, he bent to retrieve the smaller envelope and opened that one, too.

Price's jaw dropped. Inside was a certified check for three hundred thousand dollars, payable to the IRS. "Honey . . ." His eyes narrowed. "Are you sure?"

"I am. Happy life day, baby."

"If we didn't have a dime, you would still mean the world to me. Don't ever forget that."

Sable went to the nursery to check on her bundle of joy sleeping peacefully in the next room. Sensing her presence, he opened his eyes and kicked his legs in excitement as his mother scooped him up. She cradled him in her arms and assured him of her love as she whispered in his ears. He gurgled and cooed in response.

Beaming, Price watched Sable and the baby from the doorway before joining them. He placed his hand on

Sable's shoulder and looked down lovingly at his family before giving her a reassuring squeeze. Sable looked up at Price as she held the baby close.

"Ready for the big day, sweetheart?" He cupped her face and planted a light kiss on her lips.

"Yes." She kissed him back as the baby grabbed Price's ear and pulled at Sable's hair.

Price took him from his mother. "How's my little man this morning, huh? How's my little man?"

"Such a good boy. He's such a good boy." Sable stroked his head and then turned toward her husband. "We are so blessed."

"We are," he agreed.

Later that morning, Price and Sable prepared for the christening of their son, all decked out in his little white suit. Price passed the baby to his godparents, his legs kicking. Proud godfather David beamed as Solomon Dante Galore's tiny fingers curled around his own. Godmother Chantel rubbed his back and looked on lovingly.

Websites & Hotlines

National Domestic Violence Hotline
www.ndvh.org
1-800-799-SAFE
1-800-787-3224 (TTY)

Alcoholics Anonymous
www.aa.org

Overeaters Anonymous
www.oa.org

The Shulman Center for Compulsive Theft,
Spending, and Hoarding
TheShulmanCenter.com

Gamblers Anonymous
www.gamblersanonymous.org

Sexaholics Anonymous
www.sa.org

National Alliance on Mental Illness
https://www.nami.org

National Institute of Mental Health
www.nimh.nih.gov

Coalition for the Homeless
www.coalitionforthehomeless.org

Dress for Success
www.dressforsuccess.org

Bottomless Closet
www.bottomlessclosetnyc.org

Suicide Prevention and Crisis Lifeline
Call or Text 988